Obviously, Actually

Obviously, Actually

STEVE MERCER

THE CHOIR PRESS

First published in the United Kingdom in 2023 by

The Choir Press

ISBN 978-1-78963-388-7

Dedicated to Michelle and Benjamin.
I call them Shell and Ben.
Shell calls me Pops. Ben calls me Father.
They both call me Dad.

Chapter 1

North Yorkshire, 8 am. It's cold, dark and raining but I'm properly dressed and well prepared for a testing two-hour hike from Dent to Inglewood. I have driven the route before, on a road, of course, but this morning, instead of wheels, I'm travelling by walking boots, off road, obviously.

Picture me, if you would. I'm six foot six and nineteen stone. My hood is up, I'm wearing a thick scarf and matching blue waterproof jacket and trousers, with, for now, a yellow tabard. I hope I don't frighten anyone or cause reports of a blue yeti loose on the hills.

I hear the reassuring sound of my boots as I walk; audible confirmation that I am underway and making progress with dry socks. My scrambled eggs, with red sauce, obviously, are digesting nicely, and the taste of ground coffee lingers in my mouth. My hands are gloved and in my pockets, for extra protection from a wind that is becoming stronger and feeling colder than when I walked through the town before sighting the grey hills that will soon become green.

A postman bids me good morning and a rather nervous-looking schoolboy, on his phone, tells the listener that he has seen a giant.

I pass a post box, a telephone box – yes, a real red one – and a rusting tractor with a registration plate TIM 17, and think someone would pay a small fortune for that, or a wealthy, sentimental farmer named Timothy lives nearby and likes it exactly where it is.

Brace yourself, Bigfoot, I thought, as I began the climb from town to peak, where roadway gave way to path and the wind chill bit into my face. I had considered wearing a protective balaclava before setting out but I looked scary enough.

The first traces of light were breaking through the dark sky and I congratulated myself for being a mighty adventurer, going it alone, without the aid of oxygen, fearless in the shadow of Pen-y-ghent and its fearsome reputation for being a modest challenge suitable for all ages.

I thought that a prominent sign should be fixed to a prominent tree warning travellers that this was their last chance to turn back before path became grass and slope became climb. I'd come this far and, after all, it was only a two-hour journey, plus a lunch break, however gruelling, testing, dangerous and exhausting it might be. An elderly woman, early seventies, I guessed, passed me on a bicycle with a bell and a basket on it and sped – sped, I tell you – up the daunting slight incline ahead. Just the confidence booster I needed to carry on.

Now, many times I have imagined life as a farmer, but deliberately thought about the more appealing aspects such as spring lambs, building dry stone walls, working the land under summer skies and showing my prize-winning bull at the fayre. To my left was evidence, if I needed it, of the reality of winter farming. Mud, covered in more mud, with cow dung thrown in for good measure. A small herd of udder-full cows were filing into a milking shed. They were huge, much bigger than the ones on *Postman Pat*, and one of them clearly didn't want to be milked that morning. She was mooing like she was in a Yorkshire's Loudest Moo competition, which she would have won. A farmer, no doubt familiar with her complaint, 'persuaded' the beast with a gentle, almost affectionate tap from what looked like a gatepost. In she went, still mooing.

The wellington-booted, woolly-hatted farmer was on autopilot, and even though I was standing near to him at the farm gates, he didn't appear to realise he was being watched, or didn't care. He had probably been at work for two hours before the milk run (like a school run without children or a school) had begun. He was joined by a second person, who did see me, so heavily coated at first that I was unsure of gender until she kissed the farmer and no doubt wondered what was fascinating enough to cause an intrepid explorer to dwell. I got the feeling that a brief verbal exchange between the two was not complimentary towards me and possibly consisted of just one word.

I moved on, abandoning all agricultural aspirations and love for cows. I was one mile into my four-mile journey when a lone sheep, detached from a flock, stood gazing and grazing. I can never resist talking to an animal, particularly when there is no one else around, or at least not within hearing distance. The sheep looked even more detached from congeniality than the farmer had, but did, to be fair, acknowledge me by raising its head and looking in my direction. Unsure of whether 'it' was a boy or a girl sheep, I thought that I would say, Hello, sheep. How are ewe? That way, unless said sheep could spell, I wouldn't offend.

Our brief but illuminating discourse predicated on my willingness to believe that the animal could talk, consisted of an observation that it was very cold, and a joke of poor taste about a sheep or a lamb. You get used to it, was the first reply, and the second was based around a suggestion that my parents were not married when I was conceived. I deserved that, I thought, but because the blank expression and motionless body language of the sheep remained unchanged throughout, reality struck and I realised that I had insulted myself. 'Good day to you,' I said. I'd noticed that he wasn't a ewe.

Two miles in and, according to my app, 4,100 steps taken. I set up base camp beside a small cave and shallow adjoining pond no bigger than three or four inflatable garden swimming pools. Throwing caution to the wind, in a spirit of adventure and possibly starved of oxygen, I discarded my tabard, reasoning that the risk of a road traffic collision was low at my location, a mile from the nearest road. Staring into the mouth of the cave, and wondering if it housed a stockpile of the skeletons of venturers who had made it this far but no further, I couldn't resist the echo test. It fell on deaf ears, but I did achieve a sort of megaphone effect which I used to scare birds from a nearby tree. At one with nature, I searched my rucksack in vain for the packed lunch a breakfast chef had so kindly prepared for me. Crisis, I was a good two hours from civilisation and I had left my silver foil- encased toasted Yorkshire sausage sandwiches, with brown sauce, obviously, and pepper, on the hotel reception desk, next to the phone when checking out.

This was a time for my inner strength, borne out of long walks along Egremont Promenade, Wallasey, without a map or a compass, of reasoned thought, not panic, but I had them the wrong way round. I started to panic and couldn't think straight. They are going to find my bones in there alongside the other lost souls, and my tearful wife will lay flowers each year on my birthday until she falls in love with someone less adventurous but alive, leaving following adventurers to wonder why there were dead roses in a cracked vase with a note saying that intrepid people die in intrepid places and that's the way he would have wanted it. What a shame he didn't know about the bus stop just five minutes away from the cemetery where he now lies.

I was becoming disorientated, and desperate. I asked my fully charged phone, my lifeline, to navigate me in a calm voice to Ingleton, put my tabard back on to be safe, collected my bits and megaphoned the words, I won't let this beat me, before starting out on what could be the longest two miles of my life. Approximately.

A lovely, elderly, rather unsteady couple passed me en route to Dent. The lady was puffing on her inhaler. They reassured me that I was taking the shortest, safest, far-from-daring route to my destination and that my chances of getting to The Drop Inn on the outskirts of Ingleton were reasonable to good, particularly on what had become a warm, fine day. I was advised to keep going on the footpath that I was on. They had left The Drop an hour earlier and recommended the fish and chips. The chap's walking stick was covered in nailed-on badges. I didn't realise then, as a calmer walker would have, that their presence indicated, very strongly, actually, that things weren't quite as bad as I thought.

A helicopter flew overhead. It felt such a relief to know that they were searching for me. I frantically removed bricks from a stone wall and lay them out in an SOS on the ground. As the aircraft flew over and away towards Hawes, I fell to my knees, sobbing, and realised that they hadn't spotted me, due in part to the fact that I had laid the bricks under a tree and that they were covered in moss. They won't give up, I thought. They will be back; they must come back; they have to come back; they can't just leave me here. I was panicking again. The elderly couple waved me goodbye.

I pictured my lovely wife, Dannielle, blissfully wiping out my credit card in Bradford town centre, disinterested if she would have known and unaware that my hunger for adventure may have enjoyed its last meal. I tried to put thoughts of our son, Martin, out of my mind, knowing how upset he would be if I didn't take him to football that evening. Or to trampolining on Wednesday, swimming on Thursday and bloody karate on Sunday afternoon.

I tried to remember whether the sun sets in the east or the west, and, after getting it wrong, I walked back towards Dent for ten minutes until I passed a peculiar tree that I had passed earlier. The tree had been struck by lightning and looked like my hair in the morning.

I was thinking about my abandoned Yorkshire sausage sandwiches and wishing I had ordered a full English rather than a scrambled egg on toast for breakfast, with tomato sauce, obviously. There was no doubt in my mind that that young man on reception, probably on police bail, had hidden my carry-out and devoured it after I left.

I could hardly believe my eyes or measure my relief when, after 8,300 steps, I saw signs of life. What's more, I heard a train, a tractor and what sounded like a radio.

I realised, just as that couple had said, that I was going to make it. A second lone sheep appeared but I ignored it because the first one had been so rude to me, or, more accurately, had caused me to be very rude to myself. My mind drifted towards fish and chips, with salad cream, of course. What do you mean, yuck! Would I bump into the mountain rescue team, I thought (scrambled to search for me), as I staggered down the treacherous north face of a hillock, a small hill that lay between me and safety, described as easy in the best-selling Collins book of easy-peasy hill rambling.

It was 11.45 and forgetting the peril I had faced, I thought to myself, you've made reasonable time there, and you've packed a lot in, except your sandwiches. It occurred to me that I hadn't taken any photographs and that I had left my bobble hat at the cave. I had read a book by my fellow traveller Sir Edmund Hillary the night before leaving Dent, in which he recalled that he was always forgetting things on expeditions, including the time when he left an umbrella on Mount Everest. I was in good company.

I reached The Drop Inn without any sense that I had been missed or had caused any concern for my welfare or survival. There was a message at reception from The Rising Son in Dent, informing me that they had put my toasted, now cold of course, Yorkshire sausage sandwich with brown sauce in the fridge but that it would be disposed of by 1800hrs the following day if I didn't collect it. Menacingly for a little village in the Dales, in red ink, it was scrawled that the chef had made a special effort for me and that he was disappointed that it clearly wasn't appreciated, or eaten, and if possible I should avoid him if I chose to collect, because his probation officer was considering a recall to prison.

The Drop Inn had run out of fish. Apparently, a lovely old man with a stick with badges on it and his equally lovely asthma-troubled wife had enjoyed the last two. So I chose a club sandwich with Yorkshire ham and English mustard, obviously. Is mustard okay?

Chapter 2

My pride in overcoming, nay conquering, a small but treacherous stretch of North Yorkshire, with all it had to throw at me, acted as a catalyst for future challenges.

When I reached home later that afternoon, my wife, Dannielle, who was trying on an expensive- looking pair of new shoes, asked how it had gone. Not wanting to alarm her whilst she was pregnant and ignoring me in favour of Jimmy Choo, I chose my words carefully.

'Touch and go,' I said. 'I thought I wouldn't make it at one stage. It was hell up there, if I'm honest.'

'That's good, hun, I'm glad you enjoyed yourself,' she said.

I wasn't giving up. 'I thought about death, I had little option,' I said, 'and its devastating effect on you and Mathew, about my own mortality, whether my life insurance covered death from a long walk and of names for the two African elephants who I had dined with the night before, who were accompanying me, lovely lads.'

'Oh, I am pleased,' she said, lifting a Jimmy Choo heel, attached to a Jimmy Choo shoe that she was wearing, off the floor and admiring it in the mirror.

'You must do it again,' she added. Playfully, I warned that if Snowy, our jet-black Labrador puppy got hold of her shoes, he would Jimmy Choo them to bits.

Little did she know, or care, that Barnsley's very own Scott of the Antarctic, without the ice and sub-zero temperatures, was now pining to climb, hooked on adventure, excited by expedition and limping due to blisters caused by his new walking boots that were a size too big. Stand by, cruel outdoor world, I thought, prepare to be tamed. Mental note – make sure you don't leave your credit card at home next time.

*

The following day, I settled into my chair at work, logged on and asked my colleague Beth if she had enjoyed her weekend.

'Pretty ordinary. You?'

What followed was a display of, a masterclass in, the staggering powers of disinterest a woman can apply when she is not in the slightest bit interested in what you have to say. Beth and Dannielle could combine forces, I thought, and totally ignore a series of great orators, even Gyles Brandreth.

At break time, Beth said, 'It's your turn to make the coffee, Hannibal,' and I took some comfort from that because unlike my wife, the day before, Beth had at least heard the word elephants.

I was already planning my next expedition. I opened the office leave rota, saw that all of February was unavailable and, without thinking, grabbed the first week in March.

Dannielle's thirtieth birthday is on 4th March each year. The reasonably priced air fryer I had bought her was both economical and versatile, but I was going to have to buy her a new kitchen, with one of those island things in the middle of the floor, if I was to absent myself during her birthday week. Bravely, I thought, I'll put off telling her to the very last minute so that the deafening neighbour-bothering exchange to follow would last for as short a period as possible. It's normally an hour.

'You look frightened,' Beth said.

I told her that I had just put my life in danger for the second time in three days. I realised the tenuous grip I had on it and the very real cost of adventure. It was going to call for a lot of understanding and sacrifice ... from Dannielle.

Reassuringly, and in a tone betraying where her allegiance lay, Beth giggled and said comfortingly that my generally mild-mannered wife will cut my bollocks off with a blunt knife when I am asleep, when she finds out.

I knew she was right. I'd woken up on the night of our third wedding anniversary (after a similar memory lapse had created rather serious tension) to the sound that scissors make when you are having your hair trimmed, a cackling sound that only Kate Bush could replicate and a card that Dannielle had bought, and sent to herself, taped to my forehead. It was her form of a gentle warning. I would wear my cricket box, I thought, under my pyjamas when that bridge needed crossing. Thanks for the heads-up, Beth.

I swopped my screen saver from an image of Wembley Football Stadium to one of the seldom attempted and rarely climbed south face of K2. It occurred to me that I should get a few easier assents, probably many more, under my belt before booking a flight to Pakistan. I had to be realistic at this stage in my development – for now at least. There was about as much chance of me reaching that summit as there was of Gordon Ramsay giving up swearing and (not or) Meghan Markle inviting Jeremy Clarkson to a house party at their Montecito mansion retreat.

My commute home was bearable until my final approach towards the runway (or front drive) of my house. I felt nervous. There was turbulence ahead rather than behind, so I agreed with myself, unanimously, that I was right earlier and that the manly thing to do was to put off throwing myself pitifully at Dannielle's Choo-covered feet and lying about how an increase in staff numbers had left me with no alternative. That strategy was likely to backfire further down the line as D-Day grew nearer. Painfully, frighteningly, inextricably nearer. To help the reader with proportion, Dannielle's backfires are not like the sound of flatulence from a 50cc moped, but more akin to the thunder roll from the engines of a Eurofighter Typhoon fighter jet as they fire up before take-off.

I steeled myself, told myself I needed to grow up, and threw my half-sucked sherbet lollipop into our privet hedge, where it stuck to a feeding table that I had made with balsa wood and Lego for the lickle birdies. I made a mental note to locate and destroy the evidence the following morning to prevent my son from figuring out why his secret stock of lollipops had recently depleted beyond his consumption levels.

Chapter 3

Act normally, I thought, and then rejected that on the grounds that Dannielle would think that something was wrong. I bounced through the front door, did the normal just-home things in the hallway, and walked into the kitchen expecting to find her there. Her absence led to me making my way to the bottom of the stairs and declaring, 'I'm home, darling.'

No stranger to sarcasm, my darling's head popped over the landing balustrade and she replied, 'Thank God for that. I thought someone had stolen your car keys, then your car, brought the car back here, pushed the wing mirrors in, put the stolen car in the garage, entered the house, hung a coat up, used the loo and was now trying to tempt me out of the safe room with a damn good impression of your voice.'

'No,' I said, 'definitely me.' Having confirmed my identity and explained the misunderstanding to the police – ha ha – I asked Dannielle if she was dressed seductively, hoping I would engage in the role-playing game she had been fantasising about, having just finished Chapter 6 of *Fifty Shades of Grey*. 'No,' she replied, but she could have at least said *I wish*. Instead, I was informed rather dispassionately that our darling son had been sent home from school with a tummy bug and the toilet bowl was evidence of that. 'Can I help?'

'No, thanks, I've become quite adapt at working in a Hazchem suit in a limited workspace. We should be with you soon after I've checked the Geiger counter and found the fresh air spray. Poor thing, he is really embarrassed. Bear that in mind when he surfaces.'

Five minutes of *Emmerdale* had passed before my family joined me in the lounge. 'Hello, Poo Poo Pants,' I said tactfully. 'How did school go today? Did you learn anything new? Sorry, darling, too good a chance to miss, and character-building for the lad, isn't it, Smelly Bum.'

It was the 12th of Feb, two days before the anniversary of previous causes of disappointment about me. There was a chance to score some points here, and I was going to take it so that I was ahead on points when the March issue exploded.

'Let's do something nice on Valentine's Day, darling.' Silly, worthless word, nice; we wouldn't deliberately arrange anything horrible. We might do something that turns out to be horrible. That wouldn't be nice.

'I've arranged,' said Danny, excitedly, 'for two of the hunks from *Love Island* to come round midday and give me a damn good seeing-to, so it will have to be in the evening. Anything in mind?'

I was on the back foot. 'That's nice for you, darling. A birthday to remember right there.' I countered untruthfully when I claimed, 'I've bought two plane tickets to Paris, where I hoped we could walk hand in hand down the Avenue des Champs-Élysées, which is 1.9 kilometres long and 70 metres wide starting from the Place de la Concorde. Voted the most romantic location in the world for birthdays by readers of the *Daily Star*, but the plane leaves at 0830hrs, darling, which messes up your plans for lunch.' My enquiry, 'Perhaps you could squeeze them in before we leave for the airport,' sounded practical but wrong.

'Oooh, France. I like the idea of that, how romantic. I can wear my Jimmy Choos for the first time. I was joking,' she said reassuringly, 'about the hunks. They were here last Friday.'

How very funny, I thought, before revealing with a blow metaphorically equal in effect to the persuader used by that miserable farmer in Yorkshire that 'I too was joking, dearest, and I have in fact booked us in at the Chow Ping at 8 pm.'

Later, as I pulled the bedclothes over an empty-bowelled, tired young man, he asked, 'What's a damn good seeing-to, Daddy?'

Erm ... 'Mummy needs new glasses, cowboy, and the men are from Specsavers. Good night, little man.'

'Good night, Poo Poo Head,' he said.

*

The Chow Ping was fully booked. Clearly, I wasn't the only romantic in Bradford. The impact of the card and flowers was somewhat diminished by the combo being deployed on every single table. Although appropriate elsewhere for the occasion, George Michael's Valentine Classics, disco version, didn't have the same impact in a Chinese restaurant, which must have had oriental Valentine's music at their disposal.

Our favourite wine was brought to our table by a waiter of solid oriental appearance and with a broad Yorkshire accent. 'Tha knows, this is my favrit, is this one 'ere. Shall I pour, young fella me lad, or would thee like t' pour it tha selves?'

I poured and whispered romantically to Dannielle, ''Ere, get that down your neck, lass. Happy Valentine's Day.'

Do you know, after all the trials and tribulations building up to our night out, the service was faultless, the food excellent, the atmosphere cordial, our spirits were high and we had spent more quality time together than we had for months. Dannielle's miscarriage was no longer dominating our thoughts. I really enjoyed myself and I was in no doubt that my hot date had enjoyed herself too. I do like a bit of footsy, don't you?

A second bottle of wine, tha knows, the unique sound of glass on glass whilst raising a toast to one another and a second to the future. We left the restaurant laughing and a little bit wobbly, and after returning to pay the bill, hand in hand, we walked along the tree-lined Farriers Avenue, which is 900 yards long and 62 feet wide, towards the junction with Langton Lane. When the babysitter had gone, we slipped into bed and finally, and in damn good fashion, in my opinion, I took Dannielle's mind off the *Love Island* guys.

Chapter 4

The following morning, I made Martin his favourite breakfast, freed Snowy to continue his campaign of terror towards small birds in the garden and then set off on the school run (like a milk run but without cows and farmers), leaving my hot mama recovering in bed. En route, we passed an advertising hoarding featuring an image of an elderly, apparently sight-impaired lady opening her front door to an ophthalmologist gentleman and his suitcase from Specsavers.

'Is she going to get a damn good seeing-to there, Daddy?'

'Damn is a swear word, son, please don't use it. And naughty Mummy should have said flipping good seeing-to, not damn.'

'Are they different?' he asked innocently.

'Tricky one that, son. It's a matter of opinion, I suppose.' An adjacent advertisement by Ikea was easier to explain.

We stopped at a zebra crossing to allow four people to cross, Beatles-style but with prams, evidence that we were late, because they had delivered their walking-size offspring at school, on time, and were on their way home. Like Robert the Robot from *Fireball XL5*. Do you remember him? Try saying *on our way homa* in a dalek voice.

'Why are they called zebra crossings, Daddy, why not people crossings?'

Rather agitated at our slow progress, I revealed, unfairly, that 'it is because of the obvious, unique, zebra-like black and white markings painted on the road.'

'Then where are its legs and head, Daddy?' he asked.

On arrival, Miss Timkins, the daughter of a well-known, well-disliked authoritarian premiership football referee, was on sentry unit at the front gate. She made a point of pointing at her wrist watch, before drawing a yellow card from her coat pocket, making a point of pointing at me and writing out my late arrival offence on the back of it. Bit harsh, I thought, for a first offence, but St Bart's Infants' and Primary School didn't have VAR, so I was doomed and labelled a bad parent. I would lodge an appeal on parents' night. 'Naughty Daddy, I will say sorry for you.'

Another parent, apparently a persistent offender, was issued a red card (with unnecessary flare) and informed that she would be named and shamed in the school magazine. Her daughter pulled her hoodie over her head and did the walk of shame into the building. Dannielle's best friend, and fellow gate-dwelling regular Molly, had witnessed my booking from the safety of her red car and, laughing, taunting actually, was waving an imaginary card at me, holding an imaginary phone to her ear, and making a point of pointing at her real watch. My plan, unavailable to red card holders, to swear Martin to secrecy regarding my misconduct to Dannielle, was scuppered that moment when Molly began actual dialling.

Roadworks and congestion on the M6 delayed my journey to work and I couldn't help but reflect on how within the space of eight hours I had travelled from delight to a yellow card.

On arrival at work, Beth made a point of pointing at her watch, yelled, 'You're late,' loud enough for everyone to hear above the lift maintenance noise and asked me if I still had my bits.

Beth's gossip buddy Lucy, who was sat nearby, said, 'Morning, Hannibal, a little bird – named Beth – has told me that you might be a eunuch these days. You smell of elephant.' The day could only get better, or so I thought. Unusually, and worryingly, just after lunch, Dannielle rang me at work. Our darling son had told his teacher, Miss Phillips, who had misplaced her glasses, that if she rang Specsavers they would send a man to her home, possibly two men, to give her a damn good seeing- to.

I rang the head teacher to explain the history behind our son's helpful advice and to plead for mercy, possibly in the opposite order, but it did little to allay her fear that his sex-mad mother, a school governor, in fact, who was still in bed (alone, I hope) when the head contacted her at 11 am, presided over Martin's wellbeing in what amounts to a sexual drop-in centre. I hope he doesn't ask a teacher what a Hazchem suit is, I thought.

I rang the child's mother. Now, before speaking with the head, I had harboured hopes of reassuring Dannielle during the call that now the school knew the truth behind the story, they would be laughing their educated heads off, unable to teach, many looking forward to repeating it at home, and that the young PE teacher who had a bit of a reputation was searching for Specsavers online. The opposite was true. The head was minded to escalate, I thought. I used the unforeseen circumstances tactic at work before heading home. On arrival, I snapped the half-sucked sherbet lollipop from the bird table and, now dry, put it into my pocket (the lollipop, not the table).

I went in strong, confident, like a knight on a charger. Danny needed to know that I was in control and totally capable of preventing the need for a multi-agency intervention. 'We need to approach this in a mature adult manner,' I said, before taking my car keys from my trousers, revealing a half-sucked sherbet lollipop and a Lego brick.

'I know about this morning's yellow card,' said the child's mother. 'Very naughty,' she added.

Time had flown. It was already 1500hrs. 'I'll get him,' I said, and headed off to St Bart's, to get him. Before leaving, I said, 'Prepare for the return of Big Mouth, darling. He might be confused or might not even know that he has been reported. Bear that in mind, please, and don't call him the circumstances' equivalent of Smelly Bum.'

I arrived comfortably before the final whistle, but as bad luck would have it, the referee's daughter was again on duty.

I thought that if she deemed arriving two minutes late in the morning, causing her to point at her watch and then point at me, as worthy of a yellow card, I must surely be about to receive a life ban if she was privy to Martin's enquiry.

When we reached home, Martin was at the bird table when Dannielle met me at the front door. She had her mobile to her ear. 'Martin has asked Mrs Goodman what the difference is between a flipping good and a damn good seeing-to.' I've met Mrs Goodman; she would have known the answer, which would have included a fireman, possibly two, and no fire.

Chapter 5

Hopefully, fingers crossed, Martin had accepted my untruthful suggestion that the gooey, sticky yellow and orange stuff on the bird table was the result of blue tits favouring berries of that colour over blue ones.

It was Wednesday, trampolining night, currently my lad's favourite external activity. He was surprisingly confident given that he'd bounced off his space hopper when younger and lost a front tooth. He was excited at the prospect of bouncing up and down on the canvas bouncy bit, at the same time that I was considering bouncing him up and down on a surface less forgiving.

Dannielle travelled with us to the leisure centre and we watched a little nervously from the balcony as medical staff took up catching and resus positions around the four trampolines. There were four instructors overseeing activities, one with his arm in a cast, another limping, and, trying to lighten the mood, we played the which-one-of-them-was-likely-to-report-an-inappropriate-comment-from-Martin game.

We arrived home after another, thankfully short, silent journey and put an ice pack on our human bouncy castle's neck after a last-minute one-legged landing had seen him propelled, missile- like at 45 degrees, into the lower atmosphere before nosediving onto the springs of an adjacent bed, as they call it.

One of the trainers approached whilst our offspring was recovering from the tangle with the other spring and I feared the worst; what had Loudmouth said? Comfortingly, the coach told us that the not unprecedented mid-air transfer was not as bad as it had first seemed because form was important, in fact, crucial when trampolining if you want to score well, that there were bound to be ups and downs along the way and that encouragingly Martin had kept his legs straight *and* together throughout both launch and landing. Hard to see the positive in something, though, when a paramedic is fitting a neck collar to your boy.

'Aren't you two talking to me?' he asked, when he lay motionless, neckless and flat out on the back seat.

Fair question, which went unanswered, but he was milking it now, refusing to leave the car if he wasn't on a stretcher and estimating a lengthy period of recovery that would keep him off school until at least next Monday. Eventually, he was persuaded to walk from car to couch. I spotted that his legs were separating whilst he walked and thought that that was bad form.

The paramedic had placed the collar on as a precaution, standard procedure, she revealed to us, when someone who had fallen from height and may have broken their neck so badly that they would never trampoline or indeed walk again. Keep a close eye on him and check him at regular intervals overnight. Take the collar off before putting him to bed. If he vomits or gets a headache, take him to A&E. By the way, a trainer told me that technically it was one of the best falls he had seen.

Our headache didn't develop one of his own or vomit overnight, but given all the events of the previous day, school was out of the question, certainly until Monday, which pleased the patient, who was asleep with Snowy in the dog basket. We had four days to work out our line of attack. No, our strategy. I would be at work for two of them so the weekend was better, and for selfish reasons, I was able to persuade Nurse Dannielle that it was sometimes better to put things off to a later date after consideration and reflection. Good to have that up my sleeve for March.

*

The recovery went well. The following morning, Molly, the aforementioned best friend, rang to query our son's non-arrival at school. After asking her to promise sincerely not to tell anybody and in doing so break the golden rule of our recovery plan, she was told of the seeing-to story that led to the contact from the head. Unlike the school staff, in her red car, Molly put her Tena leakproof pads under extreme pressure whilst howling with laughter. A passer-by thought she was crying and asked if she could help.

'I can't wait to tell John [her husband],' she said, gasping for breath. Soon after, the same John, who I play golf with, rang me and whilst laughing his chipping wedge off, managed to convey that it was the funniest thing he had ever heard and that he couldn't wait to tell it at a dinner party on Saturday. He was a keen storyteller, and good at it. Years of breaking non-disclosure agreements had caused him a few difficulties but he was undeterred. I usually add things to a story, he told me, a bit of hyperbole always helps, but on this occasion he had enough material and wouldn't tinker with it before delivery. I could see the story on Facebook. The word hyperbole should have a y on the end of it or it looks like it should be pronounced hyperbowl, but that, as I've said a million times, was a discussion for another day. The call ended.

John and Molly are both thirty-two. John could charitably be described as cuddly, in stark contrast to Molly, who has the physique of an Olympic swimmer and a smile that can melt stone. With her wellbeing in mind, I reassess my view of her as often as possible when no one is looking.

I was at my desk, popping my left ear by holding my nose. Either I was going deaf on that side or I needed dewaxing. I had had an ear test at Boots the Chemists recently but I was yet to hear back from them. Surely, at just thirty-two, the effects of wear and tear were years away.

The remainder of the working day passed uneventfully. I logged off at 1700. When I stood up, my left knee, injured playing 5-a-side football against six men three years ago, reminded me that my ambition of duetting on a trampoline with Martin was pie in the sky and would end with me on the floor, in pain. On the way home, I wondered how my darling loudmouths had enjoyed their day together.

Dannielle's other friend and fellow confidante Louise had rung, after contact from Molly, to suggest that Molly can't hold her own water and Danny was foolish to trust her with anything secret. She added that the word promise didn't apply to Molly because she stands on one leg with her fingers crossed behind her back when she promises, in her mind excusing her from the disclosure issues her husband, John, had faced in the past. That said, she said, 'So funny, that story.'

Chapter 6

My darling mother-in-law had rung to say that she had suffered a fall at home, nothing serious, apparently. The often heated discussions about what word is the opposite of serious have torn families apart. I plumped for trivial, and there is nothing trivial about falling when you are sixty-six years old.

It was Saturday and my plans to play golf with Molly's husband, John, lay in tatters. Dannielle was going to spend the day with her mum, check that she was okay, hide the sherry and suggest respectfully that lone Irish dancing at her age was dangerous and should only be done under supervision. Apparently, as a result of her fall, her ankles, which are always swollen due to high blood pressure, resembled those of an African elephant rambling near Dent, North Yorkshire.

I helped Dannielle prepare for the ten-mile slog to her mum's domestic dance studio. We thought about contacting Michael Flatley's people to request a get well soon card from him, but she wouldn't be able to read it until the glasses she fell on and irreparably damaged during the last, most painful, stage of her fall were replaced. 'What a perfect opportunity for you to speak, boy and man, if you want to think in those terms,' she said, referring to me talking to the young man who now, at our insistence, wore headphones around the house in case he repeated anything he had heard at home when at school or anywhere else.

'Why don't we travel with you, darling?' I said, trying to delay the talk still further and fearful of doing it alone. 'Nanny hasn't seen Marty Warty, as she calls him, for some time.'

'No, stay here. She doesn't like you.'

'Well, I don't like her worse, na na nana na,' I whinged, shaking my head from side to side, 'but I hope she's okay, not because I care, I just don't want you staying down there. Why isn't your dad on nursing duty anyway?'

'Because he left her again, three months ago, stupid.' The very word stupid is an intonation fan's favourite, as you can use it in many ways, depending on your tone. Dannielle had opted for an are-you-completely-stupid tone, which achieved the desired effect.

She persisted with, 'Keep up with family matters, and don't be so pathetic, pitiful, piteous and pitiable.' I could sense that she was p'd off with me. 'Oh, and forgetful,' she added, flagrantly bucking the trend. I thought, but didn't have the courage to say, that that was a bit harsh, dramatic, theatrical, over the top but, broadly speaking, accurate.

We exchanged a brief, uncaring kiss like two frogs accidentally bumping into each other and she was gone. I returned to the house and asked Martin what he would like for lunch, forgetting that he couldn't hear me. I mimed the knife and fork around the mouth thing and he went straight upstairs to clean his teeth. No need to rush into our man-to-headphones chat, I thought. Any man will tell you that prevarication is the name of the game when something important and reasonably urgent needs doing.

*

Although in moderate pain, Dannielle's mum, appropriately named Mona, was able to walk and answered the door, eventually, with straight arms pinned to her side.

'Hi, Mum, how are you?'

'Oh, dear, I'm sorry for dragging you all these ten miles away for your annual visit.' (So that's where, or more accurately who, it comes from.) 'Did you have to use your route planner thingy in the car?'

'No need for the sarcasm, Mother. [pot/black] I was worried about you. Tell me what happened. You didn't faint or pass out, did you?'

'No, dear, I am playing, or was ...' she said tearfully '... due to play my idol Michael Flatley in our drama group's adaptation of *Riverdance*, because apparently I look more like a man than anyone else, including the men, in the cast. I was moving across the living room floor as masculinely as possible, doing that teapot thing he does with a straight spout, when I stood on my dentures and fell, luckily, onto the couch. It wasn't lucky for my glasses, though, because I landed on them, causing catastrophic damage.'

'I see,' said Dannielle.

'Well, that's more than I can do at the moment,' said Mrs Magoo, a role that a proper casting agent would feel she was more suited to.

'Well, I'm here now. Let's see if we can find that old pair you have.'

'Very funny use of the word, see, dear,' said Mona, feeling her way around the room. 'I haven't laughed this much since your dad left me – for the second time.'

Dannielle went upstairs and searched the usual places where Mum would leave or forget things. She found an expired passport, a tube of Fixodent and an unused pair of support tights still in the packet, but no glasses. 'Mum,' she said on her return, 'no luck, I'm afraid. Do you think that the bare-chested, tight-tighted photographs of Mr Flatley on your bedroom walls may have played a part in Dad's decision to leave you again?'

'Possibly, dear. He is the terribly insecure jealous type, who once set up CCTV cameras outside our front door to capture evidence, as he suspected either the milkman, the postman or that lovely fireman from number 16, or all three, of sneaking in to take advantage of me whilst he was at work.'

'And were they?'

'I wish.'

'I can't help noticing that you are wearing odd shoes, Mum,' said Dannielle.

'Well, I agree, dear, that that one is a bit odd,' pointing at her left shoe, 'but the other one,' unsurprisingly pointing at her right shoe, 'is one of two your dad bought me at the same time for Christmas, which were considered very fashionable at the time.'

Something was ringing Dannielle's alarm bells. Not Big Ben impersonating alarm bells, but bells nonetheless. The house was spotless, the ducks on the breast wall were all flying in more or less the same direction and her bed was made to perfection, but surveillance of Mum cooking a meal and remembering to turn the gas off afterwards would determine whether Dannielle would stay another day. At sixty-six. her mum was by no means old and if 'it' was what Dannielle thought 'it' might be, it was really unfair. Throughout the afternoon, a successful touch of the Gordon Ramseys followed by other appropriate behaviours and engagement reassured daughter and enabled her to hide her concern for mother under the blanket of loneliness and ageing.

*

Danny left early evening. She was worrying about Flatley's post-injury isolation and thought she might spend a few days with her mum during the first week in March. She rang home to inform that she was on the way home, would be there in twenty minutes, and that there was going to be an unholy hell of a scene if her dinner wasn't waiting for her and a bottle of wine chilling for her.

'Better add your cycling helmet to your defence against Boudicca the woman warrior, who has an ETA of thirty minutes and who is as fearless as any man, Martin. She won't like it when she sees that we have just finished fish and chips, and have therefore eaten without her.' Had junior been able to hear, he might have gone to bed but instead I reasoned that he would be grateful for the headphones when battle began.

'I'm home,' she announced.

'Oh, you do surprise me. I thought for a second there that you had left your keys in the car and that someone had stolen it and—'

'Child, open the bottle of wine. I need it. Why did you put red wine in the fridge? What have you made me for tea?'

'Tricky one, that,' I said.

As question after question rained down, I imagined how it feels to be a coconut in a coconut shy, when wooden balls are fired at semi-automatic frequency in the hope of winning a goldfish. Two years ago, I achieved my aim to win two goldfish for Martin by throwing hoops over large cuboid targets. The two fish I eventually won worked out at nearly ten pounds each, due to my sustained inaccuracy and two strangers watching, however supportively, which added to the pressure. The annoying, sporny (scouse for lucky and English for a frog laying eggs) young man in the next bay went home with enough fish to stock the Blue Planet Aquarium, which is near to Marks and

Spencer in Ellesmere Port, which is near Wallasey. I named my catch one and two, so that when one, who was swimming in the plastic bag at an unhealthy 45 degrees, died, we would still have two left.

Defensively, I said, 'But, my darling, I felt sure that you would stay over at your mother's to make absolutely, completely, irrefutably, without doubt sure that she was able to care for herself [that should quieten you] whilst watching repeats of the 1984 Eurovision Song Contest.'

Before confirming that Martin, who was wearing his bicycle helmet for some reason, had his ear muffs on, Dannielle turned towards me with that menacing stare that only I and our (previously) noisy neighbour have witnessed.

'If you don't have spaghetti bolognese with parmesan cheese in front of me within thirty minutes, I'll...' Enough said. I turned the oven on and nipped out for the cheese. Not a religious man, I said out loud, many times, consecutively, 'Please, God, the almighty and giver of all things, especially foodstuffs, let the shop have parmesan in.'

'Your father can be very infuriating sometimes, Martin, and why have you got your cycle helmet on? I can smell fish and chips. Don't ignore me, Martin. You know what will happen if you ignore me.'

Martin did ignore her. Not deliberately, but it hadn't registered with him yet that he was vulnerable without me there to explain his apparent bad manners.

Chapter 7

John rang. 'Had to tell how the dinner party went last night. Don't get arsey because you weren't invited, because it was an exclusive thank-you to my team at work for the award of a very important contract.' He continued. 'There were ten of us in total, two new girlfriends that Molly and I met for the first time and Andrew and Michael from graphics, out together for only the second time in public, as it were. It was slow to start, to be honest, until I played the trump card. The story about what Martin said at school and how his parents think it's funny broke the ice. In fact, it melted the ice as well, so that the river was cascading like Niagara Falls, during the rainy season, in fact.'.

'I don't get arsey,' I said, sounding arsey.

'Yes, you do, often. The boys at the golf club call you Narky Knickers. I thought you knew.'

'I do now.'

'Anyway, Stevo, eventually, after we had all calmed down and residual giggling had died away, we enjoyed a wonderful meal, a marvellous banquet from the Chow Ping, delivered secretly before they arrived and heated up expertly when they did, reinforcing my office-based claim that when Molly puts her mind to it, she can cook anything. Which she can't. She cooks the living daylights out of everything. I have endured more bushtucker trials than all of the kings and queens of the jungle and Matt Hancock put together. Don't repeat that to her, will you.

'The main reason I have rung, mate, is that there was an ever-so-slight, probably inconsequential occurrence which I am, almost certainly, overthinking. BUT.' Here comes the but. I could sense one was on the way and was wondering why he had rung me for something other than golf for the first time ever. 'Well, we played that *what-do-you-do* game after the chicken sweetcorn soup. My work partner Frank's new girlfriend, Evonne, a quiet, shy woman, revealed that she used to be in procurement but had changed direction to become an art teacher and that she was hoping to qualify in three months' time. Supportively, Frank, who had met Evonne at an art class for absolute beginners, added that she was his very own Élisabeth Vigée Le Brun, whoever she is.

'After the steamed vegetable wontons, we played the classic party game, *interesting things about me*. After John from IT revealed that he liked to wear women's clothes occasionally, much to his new girlfriend's surprise, Evonne said boastfully that her sister, a fellow teacher who works locally, had convinced her that teaching was the way forward for her and that she receives constant support from her father, a rather unpopular Premier League football referee who has officiated at an FA Cup final and three England Internationals.'

Oh shit.

'Are you still there?' asked John. 'I said there was a BUT, didn't I.'

Then, looking for a way to deflect the blame from himself and Molly, John said, 'If Dannielle hadn't broken your embargo rule, none of this would have happened. You need to speak with her. Anyway, probably nothing to worry about. Take care, mate.' Click.

Oh shit, shit, shit.

Chapter 8

'Don't worry, baby,' I said. 'Everything will turn out right.'

'Baby? Baby? You have never called me baby before. You've slipped up there, Casanova. You're having an affair, aren't you? Can things possibly get worse? It's all coming together now, the showering, the clean car. Why didn't I pick up on it? It was staring me in the face and I missed it.'

'Don't panic, don't panic, darling. The Beach Boys were on the radio whilst you were getting dressed.' Compassionately, and concerned about her frayed nerves, but for her own good, you understand, I patronised her when saying, 'There is a lesson here for you, Madam. Don't tell Molly anything in future, stupid [15-all], and I mean for the rest of your life, or the afterlife if there is one, or if you're just dead.' I gently pulled her towards me; she needed a hug. And then I kissed her. Thank you, the Beach Boys.

I was consumed by fear regarding Evonne's father, who was also the father of the gatekeeper, Miss Timkins. I hid my emotion from Danny – I hate to see a grown man crying – and managed to stop fairly quickly. 'I've been thinking, darling, that with a bit of luck, Evonne might soon hate her sister and could vow never to speak with her again after realising that being an art teacher was wrong for her, because the stark truth is that she is cripplingly shy and can't paint, or draw, and the nasty card-flashing [still a bit raw] gatekeeper, her own sister, for goodness' sake, might persuade her to abandon the heady film star lifestyle that is procurement because of an anticipated future staff shortage in the art department at St Bart's. As a result, the danger has passed.'

'Really, Stephen, do the Beach Boys have songs entitled *Load of Utter Bollocks* and *Cuckoo*.' Bit harsh, I thought, especially the first one, but I understood the reasoning behind her total rejection of my line of thought. After all, the entirely feasible prayed-for falling-out between the siblings had to happen between now and when they met for coffee tomorrow. With their father.

A second call from John. He had spoken to Evonne's boyfriend, his work partner and close friend Frank. Apparently, on the way home in the taxi, Evonne had given John and Molly a big **9**, which might have been a 10 were it not for Molly's indiscretion. She was not one for kind words, believe me, he had said, but she thoroughly enjoyed the meal, despite finding an order for a banquet x ten, plus prawn crackers, stuck to the underside of her dinner plate. More importantly than that, she felt very comfortable in both his and Molly's company and was keen to develop that friendship. They had agreed to meet as a four for a pub lunch next Sunday. Clearly, and worryingly for Frank, her secretive response to finding the food order, reinforced by a willingness to compliment Molly on cooking that she hadn't cooked, demonstrated that she could keep a secret for the greater good and that she was a devious sort when being so was to her advantage. He would speak with her and, flower in hand, pathetically beg her not to mention John's disclosure to her sister or father. Frank told John not to worry and that he would sort it out, even if it cost John a devious gift of her choice.

What a relief, I thought.

Dannielle was also relieved but, in my view, disproportionately disappointed about the discovery of the source of the food.

'That was your fault,' she said.

Now for my talk with Martin. I walked to the bottom of the stairs and gently yelled a request for him to come downstairs. After ten minutes, I climbed the stairs to find him asleep in bed. Still wearing his cycle helmet and ear muffs. Later, on the couch, I was prepared. I had practised my facial expressions in the mirror and gone for the look that Grandpa used to use in *The Waltons*. In a show of support for me, Danny had left for Molly's to make sure I was telling the truth about John's call.

I hand signalled a screwing motion over my ears and the ear muffs came off. Martin's ears were a good deal flatter to his head than they used to be, pre-crisis, and this would go some way towards stopping his friends calling him Wing Nut. 'Not every conversation is easy, Martin,' I said. 'You are, after all, only eight years old or thereabouts [he was seven actually], and I want to talk to you on your level as it were.'

I opened with, 'Did you sleep well then, Marty Warty?'

He nodded and screwed his face up like he does when he's confused. 'I want my mummy.'

My opening had been too childish and below his level, and I needed to slowly, carefully and subtlety ramp things up.

I attacked with, 'Some of the things that you have said in school recently have caused Mummy and Daddy nightmares. That is why you are wearing headphones.' It would be hard to defend that adult salvo when I gave Dannielle the feedback later, so I decided to edit it when the time came. At least I hadn't bottled it and buggered off to Molly's. Grandad Walton would have gone in better than that, and on reflection, I understand how an eight-year-old or thereabouts might struggle to link headphones with parental nightmares.

'Now, I don't want you to worry about it. It's part of growing up, son, and part of life that people, and especially very young people like you, sometimes say the wrong thing. I've done it, and so has Mummy – too often really in her case.' He was nodding. 'This is my and your mummy's fault – more Mummy's than mine actually – not yours. So, starting now, we are going to work like a team, a small team, obviously, to make life easier. I will be the captain, Mummy the vice-captain and you one of the other players, not quite as important but a team member nonetheless.'

'Can I be the goalie?'

'Of course you can, son.' Great, he was following my analogy. 'Recently, as you know, I was given a yellow card at the school gate, and a second yellow would get me in big trouble, so we have to get this right.'

'Was it for a nasty late tackle, Daddy?'

'Well, it did involve lateness, son, but not of the nasty kind, and it was a bit harsh in my view. If you have any questions about any subject but particularly anything seen or said at home, by your mother usually, you must ask Mummy or Daddy for an explanation, not Mrs Goodman in particular or any other teacher.' It was a late but good decision to include the word seen, so that any future claim that I hadn't been clear would be unfounded. 'What do you think then, Marty Warty?' (Easing down on him still further.)

'It's a load of bollocks. I heard you say that to Mummy.'

'That is my fault,' I confessed, 'and that is a good example of things that you must not repeat. Well done. By good, I don't mean good in a you-are-free-to-use-that-word type of good, obviously, more like well done in a story writing sense, the sort that might get you a gold star from miss or sir. I mean the sort that is a good example of something for which you should by all means seek clarification, but not from Miss Timkins. I hope I am making myself clear.'

'Miss Timkins is stinky.'

'Don't mention that to her either, promise me,' I said. 'Now, have you understood what I have said, Martin?'

'Yes, Dad.' Hey hey, he called me Dad, not Daddy. 'You mean I need to grow up,' he said, 'think before I speak and continue wearing my headphones around the house, for now.'

'Excellent, I'll leave it at that, son. Give me a reasonably high five. I'm proud of you. Any questions?'

'Yes, what did you mean when you called me Big Mouth to Mummy? And I'm seven, not eight.'

Dannielle, the parental responsibility shirker, arrived home.

'How did it go with Big Mouth, hun?'

'Well, it was emotional and very difficult,' I said, dropping my eyes. 'When a dad has to put his son under the spotlight, when his mum isn't there to support his dad or her son, it is challenging and, in fact, very, very emotional, now I think back, flashback actually. I did a great job as it turns out. I managed to bollock him without him realising it, convince him it wasn't his fault, defend your absence and conduct, explain why I had called him Big Mouth and keep his spirits up simultaneously. It was all good.'

My conduct? she thought.

'What a day,' she said. 'My period pains have eased, my worries over John's party piece have subsided, a bit, my telephone conversation with my mum left me with the distinct impression that she knew who I was, and for once my husband has displayed some, but hardly the full range of, fatherly skills.'

Bit harsh and ungrateful, I thought, the end bit, I mean.

'Where is Loud Mouth by the way?' she asked.

Later, before going to bed, Martin apologised to his mum for giving her nightmares and told her that Daddy had told him that he had caused a bit of a problem for them at school, which was more Mummy's fault than his really, and that he had promised his dad to keep his loud mouth shut in the future. 'Where is Daddy by the way?' she asked.

Later still, during a brief exchange lasting no more than thirty minutes, or thereabouts, Dannielle challenged the premise of my chat with her son, who it seemed might, or when I think about it, must have told her earlier, accurately, what had been said. But at least she did it too quietly for Sleeping Beauty to hear, although Snowy's remarkable doggie intuition clearly told him that one person throwing a pan at another person, when they weren't playing, was a sign of temper on the part of one of those persons. It hadn't been our first heated discussion, and the thirty minutes flew by fairly quickly actually, unlike the pan which struck the second of those persons. Fortunately, our couch doubles up as a bed.

Chapter 9

We had decided not to mention mouthgate to Martin before school. If he would have raised it, then of course we would have engaged. He didn't. Unknown to him, I had arranged to meet with the head at 0915. Her secretary invited me to enter her room and there sat Mrs Linton, who rose to her feet, offered her hand and made me feel at ease, given the circumstances, with a pleasant smile and the offer of tea or coffee. Hats off to her, I thought, very professional.

'Now then, Mr Cunningham,' she said calmly, 'thank you for coming in to see me.' I was invited to recount the events of the weekend. Mrs Linton listened very patiently, without interruption, as I adopted a genuinely concerned parent face, much different to the expression used by Grandpa Walton the previous day. Listening to myself speak, I felt confident that the matter had been dealt with well at our end. There was a short pause before she said, 'Thank you.' A second pleasant smile and the removal of her reading glasses preceded her response.

'By way of balance,' she said, 'Martin is a lovely young boy and he is very popular with both pupils and staff. I saw him at assembly this morning and his ears looked different for some reason. Just thought I'd mention it.' She continued. 'Children using an inappropriate phrase or, how shall I put it, colourful language heard elsewhere [tactful, more hats off] is very common at primary school age when they have no idea that words may cause surprise or offence. Although potentially falling very heavily into the latter category, and with surprising emphasis on four particular words, no offence was taken, as it was said innocently, I'm sure. Fairly sure anyway.

'Only last week, a nine-year-old in Miss Jacob's class, who had heard a knock on the classroom door, said loudly, "If that's a bloody

Jehovah's Witness, don't let him in," and that incident is currently second on the staff howler board behind Martin's table-topping and probably unbeatable performance.' We both smiled and shortly thereafter ended the most constructive, balanced, well- managed rollocking of my life. Appropriately, given my surroundings, I felt like skipping across the play yard where a group of children were doing PE.

'Why are you still here, Dad?'

'Erm, Mummy asked me to drop off a letter for the governors' meeting.' It occurred to me that my next, now urgent, Dad-to-boy chat about the importance of being truthful, scheduled for next year, was going to have to be done Molly-fashion with one leg off the ground, etc.

When I arrived at work, ready to use the word delayed rather than late, and despite the ongoing lift maintenance noise, Beth, who was supposed to be covering for me, pointed at her watch and said loudly that it was becoming almost routine.

Chapter 10

Like all great adventurers before me, I found redecorating the bathroom tedious. However, it was very close to my week off in March, and although this Saturday was utterly wasted when I could, or in my view should, have been playing golf, it was another chance to bank points. Tell me, at a time when satellites are reaching Mars, why is it impossible to get a little LED spotlight into its bed in the ceiling? Dannielle had chosen the hue. Not only was I going to be stuck in all day, I was painting the walls lilac!

Toilet rolls (like drum rolls but without a drum or a drummer) love swimming, and the bloody thing had taken only the slightest contact from me (like a professional footballer) to dive into the bowl. I fished it out and put it onto the radiator to dry and go crinkly, as experience has shown me they do. Unfortunately, I had just carefully painted the radiator with that sticky paintbrush-killing radiator paint.

And why hasn't someone invented something that cleans paintbrushes when they are covered in gloss or radiator paint? As always, I intended, uneconomically but therapeutically, to do all my glossing in one fell swoop before throwing the brush away.

*

Three marvellous, some would say rewarding, hours later, the gloss brush was in the bin and I had de-painted my hands, hair and face. Mostly anyway. Hopefully, anyone who saw me walking Snowy later, who spotted the evidence, wouldn't say that really irritating *Who's been painting then?* When they know who has been painting then, like on *Lewis* when the penny drops on the discovery of the crucial missing piece of the jigsaw. Sort of.

Martin was at his friend's house for a sleepover and Dannielle was enjoying some quiet time in the observatory. At least I thought she was. I know when she's happy silent, like when she's reading, and when she is unhappy silent, and having some preoccupied time. Just to be sure, I went into the garden from where I could see her face. I have seen that face before, eyes closed. The recent miscarriage had been our second (we don't use the word *her* second; 'it' was ours, she insisted on that). She had been on sick leave ever since and had been signed off for another three weeks until the middle of March. I decided to wait.

She had become pregnant two long years after the first miscarriage and was ecstatic about the prospect of a sibling, hopefully a girl, she had said, to complete her two adult, two children – one of each – and a dog and an air fryer idea of the perfect family. The first trimester had passed without incident and she was blooming, or so it seemed, as they say. Until.

I had no way of knowing how my lady, who had now twice lost a baby, was feeling or what she was thinking. She had sunk into a debilitating period of deep, deep depression after the first, and I was terrified, with good reason, that this might repeat itself, because I almost lost her. Sounds selfish, that, I know, but I adore her and can't bear the thought of anything going irretrievably wrong. I wanted to open the conservatory doors, put my arms around her and say I knew what she was thinking about and that I loved her more than anything else in the world, and that we would work through it together, but there was something telling me to wait. So I did.

After about an hour, during which I thought she may have briefly been asleep, she sat up, opened her eyes and wiped away a tear.

Now was the moment to join her. We didn't speak at first, didn't need to. She knew I knew, and, almost imperceptibly, she nodded.

'Thank you for waiting,' she said. 'I knew you were there.'

'Why don't I run a bath for you, darling?'

'What about the paint?'

Fair point, I thought, fair paint perhaps. It was 8 pm and she looked, and indeed was, exhausted.

'Can we have an early night, hun?' she asked. 'I need to sleep. For some reason, I am still not ready, or able, to talk about it. Do you understand that?'

'I think so, darling. But what is more important, far more, is what you are thinking.'

We rose and went upstairs. When she joined me in bed, she helpfully pointed out that there was a roll of crinkly toilet paper stuck to the radiator.

Dannielle was asleep almost immediately. I was hugging her so tightly that I'm surprised she could breathe. We had to talk about it. One of the reasons she became so ill last time was that she wouldn't, or couldn't, talk about it; not to me, not to her mum, not to Molly, her GP, or to Dr Garrity FRCP.

Unlike my sleeping beauty, I couldn't drop off at first. I fell asleep around midnight with tears in my eyes.

Chapter 11

Snowy wasn't happy. He was wearing that I've-been-a-naughty-dog-haven't-I? look that all dog owners will be familiar with.

'Sit, mate,' I said, trying to sound masterful. 'I don't blame you for getting uppity about missing out on your evening walk. I would feel the same, especially if I was a dog, probably, unless I was an old dog with arthritis in my front offside leg. However, last night's howling was unacceptable and I came down this morning with the full intention of drop-kicking you over our dividing fence into next door's garden.

'Furthermore, if you had woken Dannielle, I would have drop-kicked you over two dividing fences into the next but one garden, a distance of around thirty metres, where that vicious territorial rottweiler Fang lives.

'I know the pan-throwing skirmish was difficult viewing, but Battersea Dogs' Home will be your new home if walk disappointment syndrome (WDS) ruins my sleep again, in fact, ever again. Do I make myself clear, Snow Man? And don't give me that I-dow-na-speeka-dee-eenglish look, it won't wash. When I say sit, you sit. When I say fetch, you fetch. If I say walkies, you go nuts, and when I ask if you want your din-dins, you abandon whatever it is that you're chewing and run to your bowl.' (Do you need inverted commas when you are talking to a dog?)

No response. Same expression. 'You are paying me back for calling you Snowy when you are a jet-black Labrador, aren't you?'

One of the animals from the animated movie *Animal Farm* may have got the gist and replied, but Snowy chose not to. I slipped his lead on, gave him a cuddle, which made everything all right, closed the back door and everything was forgotten. By me anyway. Snowy tends to store things up for later use.

They say dogs have owners but cats have staff.

'Who's been painting then?' said the owner of an overgrown mouse on a lead.

'Amazing, how did you know?' was the only conversation I was prepared to share with Sherlock and his dog, Watson. Snowy was marking, in fact, heavily watering his territory and I felt relieved that we humans don't have to do that. If we did, I would have to swallow two litres of water before leaving home.

'Come on, Niagara, time to move on.'

That pair of horrible, narky, barking Schnauzers on that combo lead that meant they walked alongside each other in menacing fashion and were even more horrible because of the confidence being adjacent to another nutter gave them, approached like tandem gunslingers without a gun between them, which, given the path we were on, makes them technically mudslingers. Their owner, whom I had tried to ignore many times before on previous walkies, shared the dogs' characters and as a consequence received even less acknowledgement than I afforded Sherlock and Watson.

Hunter Snowy had spotted a squirrel and was trying, but failing hopelessly, to climb a tree in pursuit. The squirrel, who had seen it and Snowy all before, paused on an out-of-reach branch, taunting Snowy from a position of absolute safety before disappearing up into the canopy. Chris Packham will tell you that it's notoriously difficult to tell if a squirrel is laughing, or even happy, but this one was plainly laughing his or her head off and therefore made it easy for me.

It was home, din-dins and a sleep on the rug in front of the fire, whilst Snowy curled up in his bed. A bed that demonstrated his hatred of anything new, particularly if it had cost me a fortune. His den of decrepitude, and everything within it, was more heavily chewed than a spare rib. He liked it that way.

Chapter 12

Dannielle had stayed in bed and was pretending to be asleep like she did last time. I left a note saying, *I couldn't say goodbye, darling, because I didn't want to wake you.* I'd considered taking the day off but instead decided to ring Molly mid-morning, explain the situation and ask her to pop over.

I arrived earlier than usual at the office. Beth, who worked flexi hours, was there when I landed. Despite her faults, many faults actually, and irritating habits, like, well, it doesn't matter now, I had grown fond of her, respected her very much as a colleague and often sought her opinion on the more difficult work issues. If I felt the need, she was to be my listener of choice that day.

At lunchtime, she told me that I was very quiet, and the story was revealed. She listened just like Mrs Linton had done, and seemed to understand my concerns around Dannielle's state of mind. 'I'm here for you, Steve,' she said, and almost imperceptibly nodded. Later, just before the end of play, I realised that I had chosen my counsel well and that she had been very unselfish earlier. She disclosed that she too had suffered a miscarriage in the past and that she was also here, or is it there, for Dannielle if required.

'Oh, I'm so sorry, Beth,' I said. 'I wouldn't have mentioned it if I'd known that.'

'Well, we're even then, because I wouldn't have mentioned it if you hadn't.'

As planned, I rang Molly at 10.30. 'Hi, Mollers, it's Steve. How are you? Do you have a minute?' I asked.

'About Dannielle?' she said.

My stupid question 'How do you know?' was rightly ignored, broadly anyway, and there followed an account of how Dannielle had rung Molly at eight o'clock, even before my car was off the drive, probably. Dannielle had been very brief on the phone, had said that she didn't think she could talk about it but really wanted her best friend with her. Molly was already at our house when I rang her.

'Can Dannielle hear you, Mollers?'

'No, she is in your insipidly coloured bathroom.'

'Keep that opinion to yourself for now,' I warned. 'Thanks, Mollers, I'll be home at around 4 pm. I'll pick Martin up beforehand. Might see you then. Thanks again.'

*

My mum and dad had arrived home that morning after their annual wintering in the Algarve. As a result, Dad looked like David Dickinson and mum like Carmen Miranda, but without fruit on her head. I was closer to Dad than Mum because he was sat next to me on the couch, asleep, whilst Mum was in the garden. I had called in on the way home to give them the impression that I had missed them terribly and, more selfishly, to increase the chances of them letting us use their place in the sun later on in the year. For free, obviously.

'Hi, Mum. Dad's asleep so I'm stuck with you. Welcome home, you look really well.' I should have learnt by now not to raise health matters with a woman who has more imaginary ailments than someone with a lot of real ones.

'I might look well,' she said, 'but don't let that deceive you. I hate the sun, the warmth, the mosquitoes, flying, Euros and your father in reverse order, so the last two months have been awful.'

She continued. 'I have decided to let the apartment go, I'm not going through that again. The timeshare agreement expires this year so that will save a few bob.'

'No, no, Mum, you mustn't.'

I'm sure she wondered why I was on my knees, on wet grass, in one of my better suits, begging, which is one of my go-to tactics when I want something badly enough.

'Just go for a couple of largely bearable weeks next winter and book Dad into the nearby hotel's senior playgroup so that you don't have to be with him during the daytime. You can drink yourself stupid in the evenings, take your tablets and then peacefully pass out, thereby minimising contact.' Fortunately, Mum is more easily persuaded than most, more easily than anybody, in fact, and she agreed to think about it.

'You can get up now,' she commanded, followed by, 'Look at the state of your trousers. I don't like that suit anyway, wrong colour for you, and if it was made to measure, it was measured for someone else.'

I hadn't been for a pint in the Tavern for ages and I was sorely tempted, because I had an hour to pass before four o'clock. I cracked, and popped in. Manager Kev and assistant manager Nicky were there and appeared pleased to see me. Nice that, but totally understandable.

'We miss you, Mr Wonderful, when you're not in,' said Nicky, as previously instructed by me.

'Understandable,' I said, 'I miss myself when I'm asleep. I can't stay too long, guys. I have to pick Martin up at three thirty.'

'He sounds like a right character, your Martin,' said Nicky. 'One of his teachers, Mrs Goodman, was in here the other night. That seeing-to story is so, so funny. If it helps, I prefer a damn to a flipping, personally.'

I had gone to the Tav because I needed a sanctuary from my thoughts and a lager in my system. (A Guinness would be my choice in winter.)

I made no mention of Dannielle's sadness, or mine. I only had the one, then said out loud, 'Aah, lovely that, thank you,' and left, promising to visit more regularly.

Apparently, when I left, Kev told Nicky that he thought that I was unusually quiet. Nicky answered, 'He might have been quiet, but he is still a magnificent creature. That smile. The modesty. The humility, that look in his eye – I can't remember which eye now – that makes women's knees go weak, if they are standing, apparently. Just one of the many ways he has described his effect on women to me.'

'I hate him,' said Kev, smiling. 'He's so damn popular.'

*

'Hi, mate. How did it go?'

'Fine thanks, Dad. Quite a few people have talked about my ears today. Do they look different to you? Smelly Belly Saffron Parks said that I used to look like an elephant.'

'You look great, mate. Let's get home. What do you fancy for dinner, Dumbo, a tree branch perhaps? Some vegetation?'

'I'm no good at football, Dad.'

'Oh, I'm sure that's not right, son, although I was so bad at football, I became a goalkeeper. Only joking, Harry.'

'Who's Harry, Dad?' (He's my grandson in real life.)

'Everton's and England's future goalkeeper, son. I know him, his sister Rubie and his parents. People have different skills, mate. We can't all be Wayne Rooneys. You are in the cricket team, aren't you? Opening bat, no less. Well done. I'm proud of you.'

'Thanks, Dad.'

'Think about it this way, mate. If you were to judge a seal by its ability to climb a tree, you would consider it a poor seal. But, put the same seal in the sea and just watch it go. Do you follow?' His expression suggested that he might not have followed.

'So who is Wayne Rooneys, Dad?'

'One of the best footballers ever to pull on an England shirt, son.'

'Do you know him, Dad?'

'I do, actually.'

On arrival home, Molly's car was on our drive, which either meant Dannielle was feeling better or worse.

'Mummy had a headache earlier and Molly has brought her some headache tablets over,' I explained.

'Daddy [I prefer Dad], you treat me like I'm a child sometimes. Molly wasn't going to bring toothpaste, was she, for Mum's headache?'

'You're right. It was me that was being childish, not you. Now finish your lollipop. Your school cap looks a little bit too big on you now that your ears are flat,' I said. 'Only joking, only joking. Don't get in a flap.' You can't teach people to be funny like me, I thought. Well, I know you can't, actually.

I was timewasting, hoping a smiling Molly would greet us in a manner that suggested all was better, but she didn't and it wasn't. Martin went into the living room to watch TV whilst I followed Molly into the kitchen, where we spoke in whispers.

'Dannielle has stayed in bed all day and hasn't eaten. I'm worried about her, Steve, and I'm so glad you're home.'

'Molly, you have been a star today. You can stay as long as you like, stay over if you wish, but you must be exhausted and may want to go home.' She was, she gave me a hug, and then she did.

Chapter 13

I didn't know what to do for the best, or for Dannielle's best, in particular. I was trying to remember the mistakes of last time that were a part of a failure to ... encourage is the wrong word ... to perhaps enable Dannielle to escape from the repression that she found herself experiencing, whether that was intentionally or subconsciously. Whichever way, as her psychiatrist had said, that barrier, that intrinsic defence mechanism between her and his attempts to help her, appeared immovable, even for an experienced practitioner who had often and expertly removed similar barriers from other patients' minds.

I began to recall, in some detail, the fear of losing her to suicide. I'm filling up just thinking about it; give me a second, please.

Thank you. The slow, painfully slow, often heavily medicated recovery she endured. I was searching my memory for anything, anything at all, that I or anyone else did or said last time that resulted in a positive effect or outcome during that recovery that I might employ this time.

It felt a little cold, or blunt is a better word, to use the words *last* time and *this* time, but it prevented me from dwelling unhelpfully on *both* times and in doing so, from being distracted from the formation of a strategy, if you like, or plan designed to protect Dannielle from experiencing such deep psychological trauma again, and if at all possible to accelerate her recovery. Sorry about before.

First step, long journey came to mind. First stairs as it happens. How are you? is one of the clumsiest questions you can ask a grieving mother. How does she answer that when her thoughts are consumed by emotion? When she doesn't know or care what day it is, never mind how she is.

'I'm so glad you're home, hun,' she said. 'Molly has been with me for most of the day. I asked her to come over. Please don't think I preferred her company over yours. 'It just felt right to have another woman with me, particularly that woman.'

'Of course, darling.'

I was mildly encouraged by the absence of tears and the fact that she had brushed her hair. I hadn't expected either.

'I thought I might mollycoddle Martin [something Molly had taught me] until around seven and then I'm yours. What do you think?'

'Perfect. Incidentally, he thinks you had a headache and that Molly has delivered tablets, not toothpaste.'

'Sorry?'

'I'll tell you later. Do you need anything whilst I'm here?'

'No, thank you.'

'If Martin asks if he can see you straight away, what should I say?'

'Tell him, of course.'

Martin was watching *The Waltons* and I wondered if Grandpa looked vaguely familiar to him. We watched, side by side on the carpet, with Snowy, whilst Jim-Bob whittled wood and until they all started shouting good night to one another.

'Chicken nuggets and chips for two coming up, with brown sauce, obviously.'

'Can I have some bread and butter, Dad?'

'What's the magic word?'

'Now?'

'No, not now.'

'Now, please?'

'Good boy,' I said, which started Snowy's tail wagging.

I had never been more pleased to see Dannielle in my life. She had dressed and joined us at the dinner table. This was big ladder stuff on a snakes and ladders board. A ladder so big that it went over the top edge of the playing surface.

'I smelt the dinner cooking,' she announced, 'and I couldn't resist. Any left?'

By now, the ladder had an extension on it like the fire engine in *Trumpton*. Our eyes met and she knew in an instant that her appearance meant soooo much to me. A little make-up wouldn't have gone amiss but I was being picky.

'Red sauce for me, of course,' she said.

'Mummy's headache is much better, Marty. Shall we share our chicken nuggets with her?'

'No, Daddy. Everyone gets headaches.'

The air fryer was fired up and soon Dannielle was adding red sauce onto her plate. Funny, I thought, how men are much more likely to pour sauce onto food, in fact, completely all over food, whereas women tend to persuade sauce onto a plate in a location that enhances the presentation of the meal. I reasoned, quietly, and mischievously perhaps, that it was something to do with making the washing-up easier. Risky one, that, if said aloud in the Cunningham household. I realised that my spirits had lifted so much that I had nearly summoned the bravery to actually say it out loud.

I was getting ahead of myself. Calm down, calm down. Dannielle was making a supreme effort, partly for Martin, partly for herself, but, I'm sure, mostly for me because she knew I was worried sick about her. I thought about texting Molly with the news but decided against it. Perhaps tomorrow if this evening continued and ended well.

Martin was in the bath when I said, 'Thank you, darling.'

She knew what I meant.

'That lilac doesn't work in the bathroom, does it?' she said. 'It looked good on the colour chart. Is that toilet roll staying there forever?'

She really was on the road to recovery.

Over the next two days, I saw the genesis of something quite remarkable, something beyond my wildest dreams. Without medication, other than toothpaste, and with no direct help from me, Dannielle was clearly, demonstrably, positively and definitely on the mend.

Calm down. Calm down. The last day of February saw the last day of her sadness and I was so very proud of her. So was Molly, and I think Snowy was too, although he doesn't give much away, usually. His father, Tinkle, the biggest Labrador I have ever seen, was the same, apparently.

I started to plan a birthday surprise for Mrs Cunningham on Wednesday, 4th March. I postponed my plans to surmount K2 during my week off, thus avoiding the fighter jet backfire I worried about in an earlier chapter. Dannielle was so well that she rang her mum and scheduled a visit on the 1st of March, and I planned a challenging mini expedition for the same day.

'Mum has a "woman's problem",' she mouthed.

'I know,' I said gingerly. 'She doesn't look like one anymore. Sorry, sorry.'

Chapter 14

'Have you seen my altitude tablets, Danners?'

'Are you having a laugh?' she replied. 'You're only climbing or, more accurately, ambling up the mighty 300-metre-high Sharp Haw. It's a small hill if that, a very small one if not that, with steps and a handrail most of the way up. The authors of the easy peasy book of rambling decided that it was too insignificant to include in their rating system. If they had, it would have fallen within the lemon squeezy bracket. My mum conquered it last year with Aunty Phyliss, hardly the most intrepid mountaineers in North Yorkshire and both prone to dizzy spells.'

'Aah, but they climbed the easy peasy north face in a very poor time, not the treacherous west face that I face, which only has steps to assist with the first one hundred metres and no handrail, *no* handrail. And anyway, it is 357 metres high, not 300.'

'And whilst we are on the subject of taking life-threatening risks, I'm doing it on a Monday, statistically the day on which more sprained ankles occur than any other day of the week.'

'And furthermore, ninety per cent of those who suffered sprains, which can be quite painful, especially on a Monday, were on the feared west face, that I face, when tragedy struck.'

Dannielle had selected a dictionary from the bookcase.

'Stephen, darling, the word tragedy is defined here as an event causing *great* suffering, destruction or distress, such as a very serious accident.'

'Exactly, I don't take on these challenges lightly or for fun, darling. I regard them as an opportunity to pit myself against nature, to defeat it and to find a lovely spot to eat my ham sandwiches with brown sauce, obviously, and to break open my flask of coffee. It's a man thing. I understand why you don't understand.'

'What time are you leaving in the morning then, Columbus?'

'Early, before the rest of civilisation dares.'

'Around nine then?'

'Yep, around then, weather permitting.'

'I'll drop Martin off at school,' Dannielle confirmed, 'and then make my way over to Mum's. I will be home in time to collect him. Any idea when you will – or even *if* you will – return?'

'Experience has taught me never to forecast return times, darling. It might even be dark.'

'Have you got clean underpants on then, hun, just in case you have to be airlifted to hospital with a sprained ankle?'

Later that night, we settled down for an energy-conserving night of telly, carbohydrates and popcorn. I asked Dannielle what gave her the will to recover from her recent crisis.

'You and Martin, and a little bit Snowy. I'll be on pins tomorrow, listening to hourly news reports on the local radio, praying that you are not mentioned. By the way, I spoke to Mum again earlier. There is a lovely café halfway up with benches outside that does the most tasty buttered scones ever, sells some lovely mementos and, as a bonus, has spotless toilets.'

Dannielle decided on a bath during one of the advert breaks in *Vera*. DCI Stanhope was circling around the killer of a church warden. After watching the first part of *News at Ten*, I joined Dannielle in bed. She was all oily, covered in some sort of miracle, no doubt expensive, moisturiser. She felt like a slippy (but nicely formed) bar of soap does in a shower, so in her best interests, I wrapped my arms around her warm, firm, naked (sorry, sorry) body and held her tight, too tight probably, to prevent her sliding out of bed, obviously. I'm thoughtful like that.

She spoke briefly, too briefly in my view, of her concern for me and the dangers I faced the following day, before turning away onto her favoured right-hand side. She was either fitting or giggling. I felt it was far too early for me to release my now tenuous grip on Slime Woman. Selflessly, I decided to stay with it until she had completely dried out and was, I hoped, out of danger. Further proof, if you needed it, that I'm a thoughtful old Hector. She would have been in danger of a different kind if she had stayed awake.

We slept well, too well.

*

'Daddy, am I off school today?' Martin asked, hopefully, fingers crossed outside our bedroom.

'Shi… no, Marty,' I said. 'Please get dressed quickly and I'll sort your Shreddies.' A hurried departure preceded a rather careless record-breaking dash to school. On arrival, the gatekeeper gave Dannielle a thoroughly justifiable, in my view, verbal warning about speeding in School Lane and a yellow card for parking on the zigzag lines. To cap it off, Martin asked if he could use the word shi in school.

I prepared for battle. According to Danny, I have two major faults. One, I don't listen – and Two, something else. I had a funny feeling that she may have asked me to do something before I left home, but it was too late now; I was on the road.

Driving a rather compact but functional manual car in my size 13 walking boots was tricky and led to the return of the kangarooing and stalling that characterised my driving lessons and, unfortunately, my first driving test. The examiner at the time expressed a view that my instructor may have been a little optimistic when asking me to apply for a test. He added, unnecessarily, I thought at the time, that my instructor was probably, understandably, concerned about the wear and tear I was causing to his vehicle and no doubt hoped that I played an unexpected blinder on the test day, and if I did, he would probably get a few thousand miles more out of his brake pads. But I didn't and he didn't.

The trek to Sharp Haw was short, despite the roadworks on the approach. It was cold, wet and windy, but I was benefitting from my experiences in Yorkshire and had added a second so-called thermo scarf to my yeti outfit. At base camp, a parking warden collecting the fee from fellow visitors was cautionary.

'Take a bit of advice from someone who has worked this council-owned car park come rain, wind and shine and on every bloody bank holiday for nye on twenty years,' he said. 'His name is Eric. He should be here in about ten minutes,' he added before wandering off towards a second victim who was fumbling in her pockets and clearly had no cash.

Funny thing, fog, I thought, unless you have a hill in mind. I persuaded myself that it was early- morning mist which would burn off as I climbed, undaunted. On reflection, given that the weather (which to be fair had been accurately forecast on telly earlier by Carole) was more likely to freeze fog than burn it, there was a misapprehension climbing alongside me. Bugger, I hadn't put the bins out.

I had thought about using the 'easy' north face steps and recently installed hardy handrail for the first hundred metres before moving south towards the west face, but stories of cavalier, some say foolhardy, hikers taking unnecessary risks and never being seen again deterred me and probably also deterred my mate, misapprehension.

Briefly, I thought that in the highly unlikely event that I was to write a book, a descriptive pen picture of the climb might interest the residents of nearby Torton Dale and for some way beyond, probably. But I am rubbish at writing. Instead, I thought I would helpfully map the many picnic tables, with built-in benches, that lay ahead of me for the benefit of those following in my (rather large) footprints. I had forgotten my boots were too big and already they were rubbing. No pain, no gain. The first thirty minutes of a testing, undulating slight incline passed without event, and there were no lone sheep to ignore. Things began to get tougher as I neared a short medium incline. Fortunately, there was a picnic table before it and I settled down for a cup of coffee from my army surplus flask and to check the route.

The author of the tour pamphlet that I was relying on rather underplayed the severity of the route on pages 3 and 4 of a short but enthralling five-page publication by writing that you can see the top of the damn hill from where you are if it's not foggy (and God help you if it is, by the way), so just walk towards it. You don't need me to tell you that, surely?

Bit harsh, I thought. No need for the swearing and phrases likely to deter a novice. I love my army surplus flask and imagined I was on manoeuvres. I spent too long with it and its diminishing but piping hot liquid payload (army term) as the now frozen morning mist threatened. I couldn't help but notice that descenders were outnumbering ascenders by ten to one, ten to none if you discounted me. A tabarded tour guide told me to abandon all hope if I went further because if I did, I would join a long list of foolhardy idiots who had entered 'the fog'.

I reluctantly turned on my heels and ate my cheese and ham sandwich with pickle, obviously, in my all-terrain Ford Ka. With the weather worsening, I sped home, travelling just below the motorway speed limit.

Chapter 15

'I'm on my way home, darling. I was forced to turn back because of the cold and the risk of an avalanche, two actually.'

'Carole did say to take a cardigan with you if you were venturing out today, hun.' She was fitting again.

'How are things there, darling, at the Irish dance factory? Briefly, if you could.'

'You're a horrible Hannibal, hun. Particularly when you've been affected by low altitude. Broadly speaking [and broadly shouldered, I thought], Mum is good. Dad has been in touch and I think he may have a hat-trick in mind, if you follow.'

'Like footballers get, darling,' I added, 'but without a net or footballs or three goals from the same player?'

'Child. Her ankle is much better but it's touch and go whether she is going to be fit to perform as hoped.'

'Sorry to hurry you, caller,' I said, 'but I've got to go to the news in twenty seconds, and there are other people wanting to speak with me on air.'

'You're worse than horrible, whatever that is, horribler perhaps. Go to the bloody news then, Nick Ferrari. I hope it's all bloody bad news, about bloody you preferably.'

The phone went dead. I sensed anger.

To make up, I decided to set up a surprise Mum and Dad collection situation at the school. I would get there early, congratulate the gatekeeper sarcastically on her earlier disciplinary action towards me and wait with Molly, who is always early.

Dannielle, who always has to have the last say, drove sarcastically slowly enough into School Lane to attract the gatekeeper's attention and wave to her, sarcastically. However that is. Dannielle knows.

'Sorry about that before, my lovely. I was only joking.'

'Were you? My mum said you wouldn't recognise talent if you fell over it, like she had, in an Irish Canadian accent, oddly.'

There was an atmosphere. Molly had picked up on it too. The gossips that always stand together outside Classroom 3 were talking just loudly enough for me to hear them.

'That's them,' a gobby one said, 'the banana bunch we call them because they are both on yellows. No other child in the school has both parents on yellow cards. Shocking.'

Their leader, dressed in her red pyjamas with a cigarette in her hand, added, 'What sort of example is that to show to your child who, by the way, I say, by the way, was there on both bookable occasions and saw everything? Poor child.'

As much as she wanted to, especially after a day with Flatley, Dannielle's place on the governors' board would be in jeopardy if she caused a scene outside school. The same didn't apply, however, to Mauler Molly (her ring name), who wasn't carrying a card but by the look on her face was about to risk a straight red one. Not quite in Dannielle's league when it comes to withering sarcasm (who is?), she adopted a practised blunt approach that had served her well in the past.

'Leave it, Moll, they're not worth it,' I said as she marched towards the lady in red. Something told me she might not look that beautiful tonight if Molly's demeanour translated into raw violence. Which it did. I have redacted the appalling, guttural, sustained, visceral foul language that Molly favours when in feral combat. I remember asking her husband, John, where on earth she got that from. His answer, short as it was, told me.

Chapter 16

The police were quick to respond. Thankfully, the classroomed children hadn't been released yet and would remain blissfully unaware that the best friend of a member of the board of governors had been red carded for violent conduct as expected by Miss Timkins. Molly is such a delicate, almost reserved creature when not steamingly, uncontrollably, unrestrainably wild. Blows were landed, but not too many, and the matter was resolved by way of informal verbal cautions for Molly and the leader of the pack.

'Something else for them to talk about,' said Molly. 'Sorry, but they get on my nerves, that lot, especially the one I wanted to kill. I was angry.'

'Not as you'd notice, Moll,' said Dannielle, with raw irony and more than a hint of self-preservation, knowing that questions would be asked in the chamber. 'I may have to distance myself from you for a short period, Tyson, to protect my position and to put honour before friendship. Come on, follow us home for a glass of red. Just don't get too close to me in public for the rest of the month, and on reflection, best not to follow us, take a very different route.'

*

'I am kicking myself for not kicking her harder.'

'Let it go, Moll,' I said. To be blunt and brutally honest, like good friends should be, but not always, you are lucky to be sitting here with that very expensive glass of red wine in your hand, in a crystal glass, rather than in a police cell sipping warm water from a plastic cup, wearing handcuffs for the officers' safety, demanding contact with your solicitor, banging so hard on the cell door that your hands bleed and—'

'Shut up, Steve,' advised Dannielle.

'Sorry, sorry, Moll, more wine? John has just texted me, Mauler. He has heard about the disturbance on Radio Bradford. He's on the way round here. He can drive you home if necessary, unless of course he drinks us out of house and home as usual, eats my peanuts without offering me any, spills red wine on that new white carpet that your shoes are dirtying, or— '

'Steeevennnna.'

'Sorry, sorreeeeeya.'

The radio newsreader had it wrong and was over-egging the whole thing, in my view, when we listened to the five o'clock bulletin.

Breaking news. Reports indicate that a hair-pulling, face-scratching, insult-hurling, foul- mouthed, kicking lunatic parent of a St Bart's Infants' and Primary School pupil has attacked a small group of perfectly innocent and lovely bystanders, when a quiet word would have sufficed. A terrified witness and local church bell ringer told our reporter, whilst wiping away tears, that it is, or more accurately was, a lovely peaceful part of School Lane where they were and added, 'You don't expect this to happen on your doorstep, do you? I'm shocked.'

For clarity, she added, 'It happened on Mrs Dawson's doorstep actually, not mine, but she is legless most days by 3 pm and wouldn't have heard a thing. We need more bobbies on the beat is what I say.'

When John arrived, I pointed out that Molly's name hadn't been mentioned in the report and asked him how he knew she was involved. 'Call it intuition,' he said. 'The foul-mouthed, kicking lunatic bit gave her away. Red for me, please. The expensive stuff, crystal glass and peanuts if you have any left from the last time.'

Chapter 17

The world hungover snoring champion, its partner and their child, Sam, had stayed over. One brush with the law was enough for one day.

'How do you sleep with that noise, not to mention the trombone-like flatulence?' I asked.

'I've got used to it,' said John. 'I sleep with ear plugs in my ears, not surprisingly, and, perhaps more surprisingly, up my nose.'

At breakfast, a disgusted Dannielle served a full English breakfast without beans to Molly. Martin asked if I had heard the thunder last night, which covered both noises accurately, I thought.

'That will have been my mum's snoring and farting, it's normal,' said Sam, quite matter-of-fact, a tad blunt perhaps but without embarrassment. I wish you could have seen Molly's face.

Martin contributed in an unhelpful way that only made things worse for Molly when he said – 'But it was really loud, like explosions in a fireworks factory that makes very loud ear-bursting and smelly bangers.'

'Definitely my mum then,' said Sam, nodding.

At my request, Danny took Molly to one side after she had demolished her breakfast.

'Two things, Mollers. Firstly, I would prefer you to use cutlery in front of Martin at the breakfast table. Secondly, do you think you should speak to your doctor about your, how can I put this without offending, your terrible farting and snoring? I'm sure Snowy thinks there's a circus in town.

'If you don't – and you know I love you, although not as much as before you went to bed last night, but let me make something clear, transparently, unambiguously clear – you are never, ever, ever staying over in this house again. It's bloody freezing and I've had to open every window in the house.'

'I'm lucky, I suppose,' said the defendant. 'I'm asleep when these alleged offences occur. For that reason, I plead not guilty to the second charge.'

'Alleged, you say,' said the prosecuting counsel. 'Might I suggest then, trying to be constructive, that you set up a sound recording facility in your bedroom and consider suicide after replaying it.'

I was close enough to hear and thought, bit harsh that, but fair. John told me that they were no longer allowed to stay over a second time at other friends' houses, hotels in the Dales and Cumbria, most caravan sites, and all campsites north of the north-south divide.

'We rocked up at a posh campsite in Whitby last year that we had visited before,' he recalled, 'and Molly's photograph was Blu-Tacked onto the reception wall, behind the receptionist, with the words, underlined and in capital letters,

SEGREGATE THIS RISK TO THE ENVIRONMENT FROM OTHER GUESTS AT ALL COSTS. BEWARE OF AN ATTEMPT BY HER TO GIVE FALSE DETAILS.'

Molly suggested that her overnight performance at our house was probably a one-off reaction to the disturbance outside school. Husband John, trying to help, but failing, said, 'You know that's inaccurate, baby. With all due respect, even a quiet evening in, featuring gluten-free yoghurt, can be followed by a force nine gale. You feature alongside Faeroes and Dogger on the shipping forecast. We should have a lighthouse in our front garden. I have priced a gas mask on Amazon. I alert the RNLI in case it causes a call-out.' I sensed that despite his valiant attempts to sit on the fence, he disagreed with his baby and that his tolerance levels were approaching breaking point.

'Let's go, guys. Round 'em up, move 'em out,' I said to the boys, in my remarkably accurate, much-practised, saddled-up John Wayne voice.

'The hell I did. Get off your horse and drink your milk.' Wasted on the boys, that, but an independent assessor, who I had met in our local chippie, to whom I might have said Howdee, pardner, was confident that I could make good money on the periphery of a country and western concert as an announcer, perhaps, more realistically, just outside the perimeter fence, or did he say a west country concert, a small one?

My assessor, who had changed his name from Eric to Earl, not in the chippie, of course, obviously, was wearing spurs and was the only customer who had arrived at the shop by horse, as far as I could tell. As he rode off into the sunset with his sausage dinner, with brown sauce, obviously, the guy next to me in the queue who knew him, well, in fact, was his brother, turned to me and said, 'Nutter, him,' thereby significantly devaluing, publicly, the value of Earl's assessment of my fading peripheral fortune-making prospects.

Whilst I'm on the subject of sausage dinners, there is, or was, a shop in Cheshire that would fill a sausage with any filling specified by a customer. The owner, nicknamed Dog, confided in me, over two pancetta ragù with white beans, sausages and salad cream.

'Please don't tell anybody,' he entrusted, 'there are so many sausage lovers out there who are in prison, that I have been required to give evidence on numerous occasions by the CPS. Apparently, studies have proven a direct link between sausages and crime. Burglars are often arrested with sausage sandwiches on their person, apparently.'

Dog had turned down an invitation to supply Walton Prison on the grounds that most of the ingredients requested by the inmates were subject to the Misuse of Drugs Regulations of 2001, risky to source, and difficult to get past the sniffer dogs. Very few had ordered sausage meat filling.

He grows turnips now, a process that, so far, has been litigation free. That may change if the environmental people analyse the soil he is growing them in.

'Thérèse Coffey MP put me on to the turnip thing,' he said. 'I've just received a big order from the Released Prison Inmates Society.'

'He's a melting candle, that one,' said a competitor, referring to Dog, or Sausage Dog to give him his full nickname. Stan Potts, MD of Super Sausages, Haddon Road, Macclesfield, M13 BND, open 24/7, see us on our website (who wishes to remain anonymous), 'and I hope his flame expires in custody. A very bad example of how our industry conducts its business, is Dog,' said Stan.

'He has no understanding of the words well-seasoned, texture and taste. Sausage making is rightly and proudly the subject of strict regulations regarding length and girth (steady), and Dog has brought the previously untainted sausage making profession in this country into disrepute, due in part, indeed largely, to questioning the illegality and health risks of asparagus and cannabis sausages. They don't taste that good in my view, but hey, man, who cares. Since the enquiry by Mr Justice David Willoughby KC, many sausage-of-choice suppliers (SOCS) have removed cannabis and some class A drugs from their menus. And not before time, I say, dude.'

Chapter 18

'How were George and Mildred, hun?'

'Oh, same old, I suppose, darling. I got the impression that Mum didn't enjoy the Algarve very much and that Dad doesn't care what she cares about anymore. It's a long time since he has, apparently. He must be jet-lagged. He was asleep for most of the time that I was there.'

'That's sad, hun, but as long as they don't give up our, sorry, their, apartment. If they do give it up, you'll just have to find someone else you know who has one. Let's hope it doesn't come to that and that they leave it to us in their wills, ha ha, timeshare or not. Something to remember them by as long as they don't haunt it. Martin is funny about ghosts.'

I'm not surprised, that's my fault, I thought. Last Halloween's attempts to make things realistic had gone too far according to some of our neighbours, all of them probably. Edith at number 38, the now painfully thin old lady who lives alone and who may become a ghost herself soon, has vowed never to open her front door again. Her son's suggestion that she should buy a shotgun before the next Halloween fell on deaf ears, because she is deaf. We had to throw that high-quality white bed sheet out because two Fairy capsules had had no impact and the eyeholes would make sleeping on it very spooky, for Martin. And worse, I had to go without red sauce for two days.

Mum, now seventy, was in her late thirties when she had me. I was a surprise and I'm sure Mum has resented me for it ever since. Dad, now seventy-eight, was in his mid-forties at the same time that Mum was in her late thirties. That age gap persists today.

My younger brother, Phillip, also their son, emigrated to Australia eight years ago. They haven't seen him since. Just the occasional phone call. During his first month out there he picked up what he thought was a stick, threw it quite a distance for his dog, Ned, and sustained a nasty head injury when the stick flew back, without the dog.

His birth was planned and as a result he has always been Mum's favourite, despite his absence. She refers to him as her darling Phillip and to me as him. Her dear prodigal, gluten-intolerant, unathletic darling and I didn't get on very well, not at all actually, and I refer to him in different terms.

It was almost 4th April and I was still thinking, a better phrase would be struggling to decide, about Dannielle's birthday present. I thought I'd take Snowers for a walk and an idea would come to me, I felt sure.

'Walkies, Snowy. Aah, see, you understood that, didn't you, my crafty canine. Come here, boy, sitta. Ha ha, got you again, with both come here and sitta. You've got selective hearing like Dannielle, you have, Snow Man, and Molly, and Beth at work. You don't know her.'

Chapter 19

My printer wasn't printing. It was connecting with my laptop and was therefore temporarily, I hoped, a connector not a printer. I'm not gifted when it comes to things that require skill, knowledge, dexterity or craft. I'm okay otherwise.

Fortunately, a mate, Peter 'Two Brains' Rourke (TB) – (well, I know him, mate is a bit strong really if you're keen on accuracy), writes the software that controls those creepy robots that make and spray cars. I knew that if the money was right, he would rush round here sometime this month and make the problem look easy and make me look stupid, deliberately. He'll ask me that annoying have- you-switched-it-off-and-back-on question.

I checked that I had sufficient cash to pay him before texting, explaining my plight and begging for his assistance. My confidence in him plummeted when he replied. (*No problem.*) Of course there is a problem, TB, or I wouldn't have begged like that.

Famous for lying about (no, boasting is a kinder but less accurate word) the eight minutes it takes for him to walk to the Tavern from his apartment, it should only take him ten minutes to reach mine from his, a sometimes punishing but mostly downhill distance of four miles, particularly punishing on foot in the snow.

TB has been ducking my snooker challenge for months and is a worse loser than someone who really, I mean really, badly, terribly and suicidally hates losing, which is why he is ducking.

Poor man is left-handed and close to blind without his glasses on, incredibly close, so that snooker nightmare combo of poor sight and left-handedness will force me, in the spirit of sportsmanship, to target those areas. The benefit and joy of targeting is that it will make winning look easy.

Now it's good-natured, generally – well, sometimes – and just a bit of fun, mostly. But that 'it's the taking part that counts. Not winning' bollocks will spur us on in an attempt to completely smash the confidence out of each other so that one of us goes home deflated and defeated.

Sources tell me that Peter is programming robots to disguise themselves as himself, and how to play snooker.

In truth, we are well matched.

'Hi, Pete, thanks for coming over. I'm fairly grateful to you.'

'No problem!' he replied. 'I'm moderately pleased to help.'

I noticed that, wisely, he had brought his reading glasses.

'Have you driven here, mate?' I asked.

'No, walked, only took ten minutes.'

Then he said it. 'Have you tried switching it off and then switching it back on again?'

'Of course. What kind of idiot do you think I am?'

'Well, you're the kind that—'

'Please don't, Peter. I had hoped doing the on off thing would save me paying you.'

'Oh, don't worry about payment,' he said uncharacteristically, 'not too much anyway, and certainly not now. Just buy me and Helen lots of drinks, loads, in fact, and food, if we're hungry, when we are next in the Tav. I'll open a tab in your name, which Nicky will let you view, so that you can monitor how bad things are getting on the bill front. I nearly used the word control rather than monitor, but there will be no controlling us on a free night out, believe me. Woo-hoo.'

He was gone within a flash. I had run out of black ink. Simple as that.

I thanked him quite warmly, declined his offer of a kiss and mentioned tactically that I was staying out of the Tav for a while for financial reasons. Outside, I saw him sneak into his car wearing sunglasses. He had tried to hide his car behind the scaffolders' lorry that is always there.

In truth, Two Brains is very generous with his time, without charge, actually.

Chapter 20

Out of nowhere, Dannielle asked me if I still wanted a brother or sister for Martin. I should have anticipated and prepared for that question.

'I want what you want, darling,' was the best I could do at short notice, but not as good as it should have been. A doctor at the Royal had told us that a future pregnancy carried a higher than normal risk of miscarriage. I thought of reminding her of that in the second part of my answer, but it didn't need saying out loud and she didn't need reminding.

Dannielle would often drop a seed of a subject and leave me to consider, contemplate and grow it. She had not only planted this particular seed, she had Baby Bio'd it (clever that) in her own mind and hoped, on this subject particularly, that it would grow more quickly than usual in mine.

She left me alone. My immediate gut reaction was that it was too soon after the 'second time' and that despite her healthy veneer, she may still have a little more recovering to do.

The reasonably priced but non-binary air fryer was hidden in the garage and that definitely needed a brother or sister, and quickly if Danny's birthday was going to start well and my life was to maintain its easiness.

'Hi, Mollers, sorry to bother you, darling, I can't think of a second birthday present for Dannielle.'

'May I ask what the first is?'

'Of course, it's a reasonably priced air fryer, including similarly priced and very practical attachments, the icing on the cake, so to speak. They're all the rage at the moment, you know.'

'And who said romance was dead, hey?' she asked. 'That thoughtful winner is going to take some matching or, hopefully, beating, Steve. She is so lucky to have you.'

'True enough, Mollington.'

'John,' she continued, 'bought me a Rolex for my last birthday. You can imagine my disappointment. Let me think and I'll ring you back.'

Are women born sarcastic or do their mothers have to teach them? I thought.

'Hun,' said my darling, 'if you are okay with it, and I'm sorry if I am going to spoil the elaborate celebration you have almost certainly arranged, but I would much prefer a quiet birthday. I've discussed it with Molly, and Molly has discussed it with John, who may have mentioned it to Sam. They will all be here at seven thirty on Thursday. I've ordered a Chinese banquet and I'll do some chicken nuggets and chips for the boys and Snowy, with red sauce, obviously. Sam is staying over, much to Martin's delight. Molly does kick boxing normally on a Thursday but she is going to give it a miss this week. I have persuaded her to take her noisy, smelly sleeping habits home at the end of the evening. Are you okay with it, why the face?'

I saw an opportunity to fake disappointment and hurt. I grabbed it.

'Well, I won't go on about it, not for too long anyway [maybe for the following five or six lines], but it became apparent whilst listening to you there that the only person in Yorkshire and beyond, probably, who doesn't know your plans is bloody well me. Have you arranged for Snowy's pal Rover to stay over as well? Is Mona coming over, and staying over, and booked to do some bloody Irish tap dancing between the ribs and the crispy duck? Have you booked that *mariachi* band that used to serenade us when we were in Mexico to fly into and perform at Leeds bloody Bradford Airport at midday on Thursday and later at our house, supporting your mother, and are they staying over as well?'

'I sense from your answer that you may feel a bit left out there, hun, call it female intuition, but putting your thoughts to one side for now, as usual, I repeat, are you okay with it?'

'I want what you want, as always, darling.'

'Thank you, hun. You can stay over if you like.'

Despite exploding for effect externally (effploding would be a good word if it was a word), I was inwardly pleased, actually really made up, that the birthday was sorted. In a secretive text message, Molly suggested a slow cooker, reasonably priced. She added that Dannielle had spotted a *lovely* dress in Marksies when they were out shopping and that she planned on treating herself to it with her birthday money.

'I'll nip in and get it, and you can sort me out later,' so to speak. PS Warning, warning, she warned, 'It is <u>un</u>reasonably priced, <u>very</u> <u>un</u>reasonably actually.'

John rang a little later. He knew that, characteristically, I had left it late to sort Dannielle's birthday. 'You've got away with one there, haven't you, Romeo?'

'Yeh, mate, thanks for ringing, I am *so* relieved. When Danny told me her plans for dinner, I threw a fake spur-of-the-moment hissy fit, pretending to be upset, excluded and briefly annoyed, including some unnecessary overuse of the b word for emphasis and oodles and then more oodles, appropriately, of sarcasm. Have it, Peter Kay fashion, a bit of her own medicine, so to speak, ha ha. She was completely taken in. Hook, line and bloody sinker, it was brilliant. Ha ha.'

At that moment, a cup of tea slid very slowly onto the coffee table. I hoped that the saucer had learnt to walk on its own. But no.

'Been there long, darling?' I asked in a squeaky voice.

She had been there long. Behind me and out of sight. I had put my feet on the coffee table and she revealed, knowingly, that she had been waiting impatiently for the full duration of the call for me to remove said feet, before putting the cup down.

'Hook, line and bloody sinker, eh?' she said. Yelled actually.

I would have preferred her not talking to me for a punishing, suitable length of time, perhaps until the Chinese food arrived in two days', to what I actually found myself on the receiving end of. On the grounds that some delicate, easily upset, sensitive and sarcasm-hating sorts might be reading, I'll leave it there.

Chapter 21

On the day before Dannielle's birthday, I found myself alone in my study, not surprisingly, locked inside it actually, for my own safety. Molly had rung her. Apparently, she had blown the secret about the surprise dress present and had invited Dannielle to pop into Marksies with her to collect it. It would be good idea to try it on first, I thought.

My optical wired computer mouse with easy click for office, home (and study) use, premium, portable and compatible with my PC, had landed and to add to my excitement a second parcel brought a non-slip, rubber base desk mat. The courier, standing a good bit further back from the door than other couriers had before her, told me that she had tried to deliver the parcels the previous evening, but the mad woman who opened the front door had told her she could stick them up her arse and slammed the door shut.

'I'm awfully sorry,' I said, and told her that that would be my darling wife, who is a complete nutter when it comes to parcels and that she was annoyed with me over something trivial.

'She is very sensitive to trivial things,' I added.

'Well,' the nervous young lady replied, 'I'm going to trivially hurl your parcels into your front garden in future, and I will be hoping that they land on your black dog's poo.'

'That would be Snowy,' I informed, confusing matters.

My neighbour Bill was passing. 'Is everything okay?' he enquired.

'Of course, old man, it's just the delivery of my compatible mouse and rubber base mouse pad.'

'No, I'm not talking about that. Incidentally, I saw a young delivery lady running from your garden fence to her van in tears yesterday. Anyway, no, I'm talking about yesterday afternoon when either you had captured a notoriously noisy and vicious Tanzanian warthog or you were getting the living shit kicked out of you. The screams, although a bit girly, very girly actually, were definitely yours, and it was so bad at one stage that it sounded like an unhealthy, prolonged hog- and shit-kicking combo was underway. Now, concerned about you, I asked the wife if I should phone the police. She was a little reticent, if I can put it that way, when she said, "No point, they – the police – have stopped attending calls about next door, my last two calls anyway."'

'*Jurassic Park 3*, Bill,' I claimed.

'What?'

'Sorry, old boy, I was watching part three of *Jurassic Park*, with Martin and Snowy, the three of us, fittingly.'

'Ooh, I didn't know they were in it,' he said. 'Who'd have thought I would have two of the cast of a blockbuster living next door. I must get the videotape. I've noticed that your lad wears headphones at home nowadays. That makes sense now. Please have a little twist of the volume switch next time you watch a film, Steve.'

After checking it was safe to do so, I went into the lounge and selected the dictionary that Dannielle had employed to mock me, unmercifully, but effectively, two days earlier. I read, *easily persuaded to believe something incredulous or unbelievable.* Helpfully, a suggestion of how you use the word gullible in a sentence was available. *That old man Bill next door is gullible.*

Chapter 22

Late afternoon, Dannielle was home and in the kitchen. I could sense her presence from my hiding place. An icy cold blast permeated my locked door. I felt like I was playing hide and seek without someone seeking. I heard the sound of Snowy's metal food bowl sliding around on the kitchen floor as he hoovered up the last morsels. Snowy, Frosty and an icy cold in the same room, I thought. I was bound to get the cold shoulder when I had the courage to join them. Funny that. I had to face her sooner or later, and I hoped that the icy blast would slowly subside to be replaced by an atmosphere of forgiveness and reconciliation.

I left my cell and wondered why I was tippy toeing towards the walk-in fridge that was masquerading as a kitchen. I had oiled the hinges on every one of our internal doors recently as part of a maintenance drive, but the kitchen door made that creaking, ghostly sound as I opened it. Snowy abandoned his bowl and hid behind a table.

Helpfully, Agent Orange, John, had texted me earlier to report that Molly had mentioned that Dannielle's mood had improved whilst shopping. Nothing new there. She had sworn Molly to secrecy in Marksies when confiding in her that she planned to ease off on me because I had been very supportive recently, and that she didn't want to miss out on the Chinese, or risk having to pay for the new dress herself, or jeopardise finding out what lurked in wrapping paper, below the tins of paint, in the garage.

True to form, Mollers broke Dannielle's trust at the first opportunity and John was good enough to give me the heads-up. He had the same attitude as his darling kick boxer towards secrets and felt no remorse about alerting me. Buoyed by my informant's contact, my spirits had lifted from desperately low to just below average.

'You okay, darling?'

'Yes, thank you.'

Not her warmest tone, but at least we were talking. Snowy bravely returned to his bowl. The evening was spent making incremental improvements in the atmosphere. My joke that we should choose chilli for dinner drew one of those looks, but no answer. At least we were looking at each other.

By early evening, thanks in part to Martin joining us and partly due to Dannielle's hope that he wouldn't sense things weren't exactly good between us, when they exactly weren't, the atmosphere was a little improved. Bit by bit, though, as the thought of losing that far-from-reasonably-priced adornment struck home, relations improved sufficiently, on her terms, obviously, to give grounds for hope that Birthday Day was going ahead. I began to prepare for bed knowing that I was not allowed to touch, not yet anyway. History had shown that when everything was going her way, Dannielle rather liked being touched whilst in bed, absolutely loved it actually. So much so that I had learnt to target her non-erogenous bits when nervously giving her a pre-sleep good night touch, if I was going to be left alone to doze off.

Chapter 23

Inside the large pink envelope that I was handling lurked a ridiculously expensive birthday card. I had chosen it a week earlier when my feelings for the intended recipient were Premiership, not Conference. Now, as my thoughts were fighting a relegation battle, I was so tempted, sorely so, to tear open the seal and write the words, '*but not always, unfortunately*', behind the '*wonderful*', thus making the message '*To my wonderful wife, but not always, unfortunately*'. I knew that grammatically it was poor, because it also suggested that Dannielle isn't always my wife. I resisted, but only just, before sellotaping it onto the top of the box containing the air fryer.

Wednesday, 4th March was with us. The cold war was enjoying, or more accurately enduring, a fragile ceasefire, but both sides remained on the alert, with metaphorical troops at the borders (more on mine, with more tanks), guarding against a resumption of hostilities.

My troops were understandably less optimistic and more terrified than their opposition, who were safely entrenched a short, too short really, Ronnie Corbett sort of short, distance away from them.

Breakfast was quiet but bearable and soon after, Muffs and I were on our way to school.

'Daddeeeey.'

'Son.'

Mummy isn't very happy on her birthday day, is she. When she opened the box with that food cooking thingy in it, she used a word that I am damn sure I can't use in school, hee hee.'

'Three points there, son. First one or firstly, as you already know, damn is on the not-to-say list, for you anyway. Second or secondly, the food cooking thingy is a versatile addition to any kitchen, and number three, don't worry about your mummy, she has an unusual, some would say irritating, well-camouflaged way of showing that she is enjoying something, and before you ask, camouflaged means unfair when used in this context, in a hidden, difficult-to-see kind of unfairness.'

I wished he was dropping me off at school rather than the other way around.

He asked what context meant. I explained that it was one of those words that needed to be used at the right time, and I gave him permission to use it in school. Not helpful on reflection.

On my arrival back home, after taking the longest route, Dannielle was displaying clear symptoms of a split personality. In a room where she had shown scant regard for my life only seventeen hours earlier, she had a full English in the oven for me, which would have been much less dry, or rigid is better, if I had taken the normal route home. I had a missed call from my mother. I would ring her later, after I had found out if I was, relatively speaking, off the hook or whether I was going to be subjected to a punitive set of plans intended to wipe millions off my self-worth rating. I had decided to be non-compliant, but only briefly.

I poured on absolutely loads of brown sauce, obviously; so much, in fact, that only our dishwasher at its highest temperature setting would have a hope of shifting it later. If I'm honest, the poached eggs were so dry that it was like chewing two golf balls, but I was complicit and took my medicine, well, my eggs. They, and particularly the really round one, reminded me that I hadn't played golf for some time, and the other one made me think that the process of laying an egg must be very uncomfortable.

I reasoned that Dannielle's undoubtedly well-thought-through plans to punish me (the more likely of the two courses of action outlined above) were based on a prophecy she relied on when defending a decision, a knee-jerk one in my view, to banish Martin to his bedroom without any dinner after drawing on the wallpaper aged five (for clarity, he didn't write the words *aged five* on the wallpaper, are you with me?), most of the wallpaper, actually, and on another occasion, me, to our bedroom without lager, for breathing, as far as I could make out.

I remember her saying at the time, 'People will not stop doing naughty things if you don't punish them, often seriously, in a way relative to the naughtiness committed.'

I was sitting watching television with Martin and Snowy on our return from school that day when I spilt coffee on the carpet.

'Could mean the bedroom, Daddy.'

Snowy, listening carefully, had spent most of his time as a naughty puppy being thrown in, sorry, no, returned to *that bed* in a plan designed to stop him doing something naughty, again. The remainder of his puppyship demonstrated that he couldn't link being naughty with being launched into his bed. Love him, though.

'Did Mummy not like the cooking thingy, Daddy?'

'Deep down, possibly, son. You were at school when she discovered the attachments and saw the endless opportunities for safer transference of food from the food thingy to a plate, not to mention flipping pancakes and other egg-based flattish stuff. I also gave her a lovely dress that she had worn before.'

'Molly told me about the dress yesterday, Daddy.'

The same Molly, who had felt a little pent-up without fellow parents available to beat up, had attended an earlier kick boxing class. John had rung to ask me what Dannielle's favourite bottle of wine was, and I told him, an open one, which is next to a full one. Molly had returned from the ring in a more mellow mood, apparently. But John added the caveat that she was still prone to going off like a Roman candle, a large missile-like candle powered by a throaty Catherine wheel, if provoked, so he advised me to stay off the subject of dish washing and its origins from when men were out hunting, etc.

The banquet for four with prawn crackers had arrived, and our guests were en route. An enclosed message from someone named Arthur Wong read, *Tha knows, lass, me antuthers 'ere, not all ovem mind, bein brutally on-est, would like to wish you an 'appy birthday.* The defences were down and Dannielle said, 'Aah, how lovely.'

(I withdrew some but not all of my metaphoricals from the border.)

'I wonder how the Chow Ping knew it was my birthday.'

I explained that I had rung them to ask that no form of identification whatsoever be included in the wrapping of banquet C for four with prawn crackers, so as to avoid a repeat of the awful occurrence and discovery at John's recent, exclusive *workmate only, mate* dinner party.

'But John and Molly know we've ordered it,' she said.

'I'm just trying to set a precedent so that we don't have to go through it every time we order when our guests are from work and I've told them you are Bradford's most credible threat to Ken Hom.'

I discovered later from my metaphorical troops, well, from one of them, actually, a fearless former assistant scout pack leader, that Dannielle's army had adapted a rather *laissez-faire* attitude to the standoff. They too had ordered Chinese with prawn crackers but for an estimated 200 (including seven vegetarians and a vegan apparently), plus a sixteen-strong civilian support team who were playing badminton. Music played courtesy of their very ordinary-sounding military band as the unmistakable and criminal smell of cannabis drifted in the air on the moonlit night as stars maintained their celestial watch over them and drifting, really-difficult-to-see clouds meandered above like they do in the daylight but when you can see them clearly. And nearby, cattle and sheep, stood almost motionless, were lowing in a stable that was next to a hotel that had no vacancies.

Upstairs, Sam and Martin were being mischievous over a very close game of draughts. Martin was playing with the blacks and Sam with the whites.

'Damn good at this, aren't you, Sam? You could be a champion in about ten years when you are a bit more growed up.'

'Don't talk bollocks,' said Sam, before they both put their hands to their mouths and giggled. Nearly died laughing, actually, particularly Martin, whose condition was described as critical at one stage. Sam clearly didn't have headphones at home. That was his birthday present sorted.

On the floor below them, I winked a further thanks to Agent Orange. MFI would be proud to have him, although his name would no longer be John. Molly presented Dannielle with an expensive bottle of perfume and a slow cooker. John quietly asked how my day had been.

'Awful and therefore much better than I expected,' I said, before we copied the boys but with a mouth-covering bout of uncontrollable laughter.

'Something funny?' asked Molly.

'Nothing gets past you, Vera,' I said. 'How did you know we have found something funny? Where did we make that one mistake that most criminals make before their arrest and subsequent conviction, sentencing and incarceration and much later, release?' I asked.

'Well, that was an unnecessarily long question for a start, and given that an agent is involved, I have to be careful what I say,' said a now wine-affected-soon-to-be-wine-afflicted Dannielle.

'Do you know the difference between MI5, who I assume you were thinking about earlier, and MI6?' asked Molly. Hic.

'No, but I know the difference between MFI and Bensons for Beds now,' laughed John. (Hands to mouths, etc.)

Undeterred, Molly continued – 'MI5 deal with home security and MI6 with foreign bodies, something a real agent would know, actually.'

'I've blown my cover there,' said John. 'The MI6 guys weren't there when I got a foreign body stuck in my throat and nearly choked to death, were they?' he asked. 'No.'

I added, 'They were probably stuck on the motorway near to the Sandbach Service Station on the MI6.' (Hands to mouths, etc.)

'There are four children in this house tonight, children,' was the birthday girl's retort.

The beer was taking effect, quickly actually, and John's brain was morphing into the sporto-cerebral equivalent of a rainsoaked pitch. Soon his jokes would be more suited to an audience without moral compass, as always. I was left wondering how Molly had managed to hear something I was only thinking earlier. No wonder John doesn't think much, if at all, I thought. Molly gave me a knowing look for some reason.

Do you know, we had a lovely, lovely night.

Later, after Molly had taken her bad habits home, John's rainsoaked pitch had led to it being unplayable and Jedward had fallen asleep, I was less than careful where I touched Dannielle.

Chapter 24

The following morning, I remembered that I had forgotten to ring my mum back.

'Hi, Mum, sorry I didn't ring you back yesterday, Dannielle's birthday and all that. How are you?'

'I'm fine, son. Second favourite son, actually. I'm ringing about your dad. He was asleep for most of the time on the day we arrived home from the Algarve, so you may not have noticed.'

'Noticed what, Mum?' I asked.

After a short pause – 'Our holiday was horrible and not least because he is horrible sometimes. Twice … twice … he forgot where we were staying after going for walks. He had been out far too long the first time and I found him outside a bar on the seafront, with a waiter running through a list of nearby hotels in the hope that he might recall where he was staying. I let him put it down to a touch of sunstroke. As a precaution, I wrote the hotel name on a piece of paper and put it in his wallet. A waiter from another bar brought him back to me on the second occasion.'

'How has this come on so suddenly?' I asked.

'It hasn't. You don't exactly over visit, do you, or you would have seen it.'

Gulp.

*

Later, at the coffee shop, she continued. 'I'm worried, Steve. I worry about looking after him and feeling sorry for him in equal measure. He had bloods done yesterday. I know what the results will be. There is no point me thinking that it will pass. I used to kid myself with that at first but not anymore.'

Mum was struggling, so I hugged her, she needed it, and obviously, she will need many more in the future. I wished I had given her more in the past. Many more, actually.

'I feel helpless, son.'

'Come on,' I said, 'let's go home and I'll talk with him.'

'No, I'll stay here and walk home in about an hour. It isn't far.'

I rang the doorbell. 'Dad, are you there, can you hear me? Open the door, please, Dad. Thanks. How are you, old man?'

'Fine.'

In the lounge, I looked closely into his eyes for the first time in a long time. They had that slightly distant look in them like his late elder brothers had as dementia took hold.

'How are you really feeling, Dad?'

'Fine, why?'

'Mum tells me you are getting a bit forgetful, Dad.'

'I'm seventy something.'

'How did the holiday go?'

'Fine.'

'What was your hotel like?'

'Fine.'

'And the food?'

He wasn't looking at me. 'Any problems out there, Dad?'

'No, not that I can remember.'

'I remember Dannielle getting a little tipsy in Cyprus once, Dad. We couldn't remember where our hotel was until we woke up the next morning on the beach, ha ha. Has anything like that happened to you?'

No response.

'Did anything at all happen to you out there, Dad?'

'No.'

Dad has never called Mum anything other than by her name, Alice, until now.

'Where is, oh, what's-her-name, it'll come to me in a minute ... my wife, where is she?'

'What did you have for breakfast, Dad?'

'When?'

'This morning.'

'Erm, hang on, hang on. No, it's gone.'

So I hugged him; he needed it. I was still hugging him when Mum arrived home. I couldn't speak with her at first and hid my face so that she couldn't see my expression and the tears in my eyes. Dad had fallen asleep.

'He's always asleep, son.'

I composed myself, partly, sufficiently enough anyway to tell Mum that, as she knew, she was right about Dad.

Looking closely into her eyes for the first time in a long time upset me; the utter despair, sadness and helplessness that she had mentioned were tied up in a bundle right there in front of me, and I started filling up again. Crying, actually, like a nineteen-stone baby. So, my mum hugged me; I needed it.

We stood together watching the most important man in our lives sleeping. He wasn't the same man now but he was still the most important.

'I'm worried about my future, Steve. I'll make a nice cup of tea.'

On the way home, I thought how unfair it was on me, having only just got over our miscarriage and now having to face this incurable bastard disease that had my dad by the bollocks.

I recalled John's pal Frank telling me how his grandad had suffered.

'It robbed a very proud man of his dignity, Steve,' he had said. 'He hardly had two pennies to rub together in his entire life, but he would look immaculate twenty-four seven [now smiling], even in his pyjamas.

'He left the house one morning with food all over the front of his vest, no teeth in and odd shoes on. People who hadn't seen him for a while didn't even recognise him. The police found him, cold and disorientated on a park bench.'

It had upset Frank that people had walked past his clearly vulnerable grandad and hadn't stopped to enquire. The insidious slow creep was unbearable to watch, he told me, both by them and by the nurses in the care home who liked and cared for him, and had seen it all before.

'Grandad couldn't remember his wife's name for about a year before he died. He couldn't remember his own, or anything, in fact, in the six months before he left us.' His wife, Sally, stopped visiting soon after he went into care. Her husband, who was alive but had died a long time ago, was so ill that she could no longer bear seeing him. She felt awful for not visiting until, and during, a phone call from a staff nurse at the hospice where he spent his last two months. She learnt that one out of five people in their care died alone for that reason, which helped and didn't help.

Although selfishly feeling sorry for myself, I felt so sorry for Dad, and even more sorry for my mum, who might soon be nursing a stranger that she had been married to for over forty years.

Chapter 25

I was bladdered. The two-bottles-of-red-with-plain-crisps, obviously, type bladdered; the emotionally brittle, totally-consumed-by-your-thoughts kind of bladdered that meant you shouldn't attempt trying to talk to anyone, or walking a great distance, any distance, actually. I had told Danny about the situation earlier. A doorman 'informed' me that I couldn't have another drink, let alone another bottle of red. Harsh but fair, I thought.

Dannielle picked me up. 'I'm hurt that you chose alcohol over me this evening. I thought those days had passed.' I also thought that those days had passed, but evidently not. It's fair to say that I'd leant on alcohol in the past.

'Everyone has to face old-parent problems, Steve. It's part of growing up, or part of getting old from your dad's perspective.'

'You're right, darling.'

In my foggy mind, I had mental pictures of Mum and Dad, and in my ears, I could hear Mum's voice telling me that I didn't over visit them. I was more upset by what I'd heard than what I'd seen.

Martin was in the back seat, so the short journey home was conducted in silence, in contrast to my hesitant climb upstairs and my falling into, or more accurately onto, the bed, before falling asleep, partially clothed.

*

Next morning, at a partially conscious breakfast table, Martin told me that his mum had rang Molly soon after we had returned home from the pub, before asking me for permission to use the phrase pissed as a rat in school.

Thank goodness it was a Saturday. I wasn't fit to drive, or walk, actually.

'You were as pissed as a rat last night, hun.'

'I know, Martin has just told me. Why wasn't he wearing his ear muffs when we got home last night, and perhaps more importantly, why on earth did you tell Radio Molly? Haven't you learnt? I'm fully expecting John to ring me now.'

'How did you know I told Molly?' Danny asked.

'Martin has just told me,' I replied.

'Because,' she continued, 'we act as each other's comfort blanket, that's why, and it was your fault you were totally bladdered, not mine.'

'Daddeeey—'

I cut him dead. 'No, you can't say totally bladdered or pissed as a rat in school, especially if Mrs Linton is near to you, and put your muffs back on whilst your mum and I have a slanging match. Do we have any paracetamol in, darling?'

Later, as I faced the man in the mirror, I looked deeper into my own eyes than I had done for a long time. I hadn't used my brain's how-to-look-after-your-elderly-parents section recently, for ages, if ever actually, and I had to rely on the 'forgot your password?' facility to access it. I cut myself whilst shaving.

I chose the password, *mumandad*, and opened up Section 2, Subsection a) which is an 'ask yourself these questions' module. I have printed them out for you.

What are the dates of your parents' birthdays?

Have either of your parents raised the issue of your prolonged absence from their lives?

How many times have you visited them in the last two years?

How many times have they visited your house during that period?

Does a sibling(s) who lives closer to your parents than you fulfil the visiting role?

Is the distance between your house and your parents' house a contributing factor? Tick the most accurate distance from the following list. 1 mile; 10; 50; 100; 150; 200; 250; Different country.

When did you last ring one of your parents?

When you last saw them, did either show signs of illness that you had missed because of your absence?

The questions in Subsection 2b) were harder to read and harder to answer, actually. Before tackling them, I was instructed to imagine that both of my parents had passed away.

Do you feel any guilt regarding your poor attention towards your late parents in the period specified?

If the answer to Question 8, Subsection 2a) is Yes, my dad wasn't my dad anymore, then how lonely do you think his wife, your mum, had felt during the specified period?

Do you think that your mother understood why it took the discovery of your father's dementia to cause you to refer to Section 2, and only after she asked you for help (and support) because she feared the future?

Subsection 2c) comprised two questions only.

If there is a kingdom above the clouds, how do you think they will welcome you?

How do you feel?

'You're very quiet, hun. Deep in thought or still hungover?'

I was both.

'I was thinking yesterday,' she added, 'that you haven't mentioned your brother Phillip for ages. Have you heard from him? I remember your mum was heartbroken when he left for Australia. Does he keep in touch with them? You didn't seem at all concerned at the time. I put that down to the favouritism thing.'

Dannielle, more appropriately named The Mysterious Danniella, was clearly a psychic, I thought, or, and perhaps more worryingly, Molly had taught her how to listen to my thoughts. If she has, Dannielle would soon be left in no doubt as to what I thought of my brother. He left for Australia to escape criminal debt, not to breed koalas.

Chapter 26

I needed a man chat.

'Hi, John, are you free for golf tomorrow?'

'Is the Pope Catholic, does a dog lick its own balls because it can, do leaves—'

'John, are you free, for goodness' sake?'

'Oooh, okay, Narky Knickers. It will have to be in the afternoon, though, Tiger. Sam has karate in the morning. Is Martin going?'

'Yes,' I said, realising that I was betraying how I was feeling on the phone.

John continued. 'Molly's parents are round for lunch *again*, no peace for the wicked. I prefer Sunday lunch at their house because her mum does world-class roasties. My mum used to buy them in without telling me, but I knew and so did Dad. He still talks about it. If I was a doctor, I would prescribe roasties ahead of drugs. Now, I would like you to eat four fluffy middled, crispy edged roasties every Sunday with vegetables. The pharmacist could have a shelf, next to the dental section, displaying nutritious vegetables. Sam once said that he will eat anything healthy except vegetables and fruit!'

'Okay, finally, sorry to interrupt,' I said, deliberately interrupting, 'I'll see if there is an afternoon tee time and I'll get back to you.'

'Oooh. You need some roasties with thick gravy, Stevo.'

I rang the club professional, another John, but a normal one.

'Hiya, Steve, I haven't seen you in ages, mate. Yes, I have a fifteen hundred start if that suits. It's the only free tee time, actually. You are lucky.'

'Great, that's perfect. I'll take it, please, John. It's a two-ball.'

'Oh, be good to see you, mate, but wait, is your membership still live?'

'Yes,' I answered, 'but only just.'

'Who are you playing with, mate? Not my namesake, I hope.'

'Yep, the phantom sand wedge flinger.'

'He's a cheat, mate, who always carries a spare ball in his pocket, bad form. I had to warn him after a dubious victory over the club captain.'

'Well, he is competitive but—'

'Competitive, my arse, he's a cheat.'

I texted *15:00 at the first and don't be late* to the cheat.

He texted back, *Oooooooh, prepare yourself for a damn good seeing-to, lol, still makes me laugh that – Narky Knickers*

'Child,' I said, out loud.

*

Martin had difficulty counting from one to ten in Japanese, generally considered a prerequisite if you are to wear a karate suit effectively and with any hint of menace. However, he made up for it on the *dojo* (the mat). It was the longest period in every week that he had to exist without a phone in his hand. He had learnt the hard way that the *sensei* (the instructor), who was a tad unhappy with him for fighting one-handed whilst killing Martians on his Samsung, made an example of him by folding him in two, origami-fashion, in front of his peers. I wasn't happy but felt that there was little to be gained by me mentioning it to the 6th *dan*, former UK heavyweight karate champion.

It was a pleasant March afternoon when battle commenced at the tee.

'Sorry I was a bit snappy yesterday, mate. I'll explain later when we are searching for our lost balls in the rough.'

'No problem.'

There it was again, no problem when there was one. We were both a little wayward from the tee. I waywarded left and John right. This made conversation difficult because our crucially important, confidence-critical first shots had landed nearly fifty yards apart from one another, having posed no threat to the fairway but considerable risk to a greenkeeper, who has worn a bright yellow safety hat at work ever since.

It wasn't until the 6th that our tee shots landed close to one another on the fairway and we could chat en route towards them. (In fact, the 6th was the first time either of us had troubled any fairway with our tee shots.)

'Mate, I got totally bladdered on Friday night. Two-bottles-of-red-with-plain-crisps bladdered.'

'I heard. Salted peanuts as well, apparently. Molly told me after a call from Dannielle.'

Of course she did.

'And Martin may have mentioned it to Sam at karate.'

Of course he did.

'Martin told Sam that he thinks his dad was sucking one of his secretly stored lollipops and that he was very wobbly.'

'Aargh, Marty knows. Do you need me to go into detail about why I got bladdered, etc., or are you fully briefed?'

'Briefed enough to listen, Stevo. Fire away.'

'I have been ignoring *them,* busy life and all that. Not a deliberate purposely-avoiding-them type of ignoring them but ignoring them nonetheless.'

'Excuse me. Point of order, Stevo. Try not to use the same word three times in one important but relatively short sentence or you may lose my brittle interest. Basic English Lit. Have you noticed by the way that yellow hat wearing has become policy for the ground staff? It looks like a *Bob the Builder* convention around here. Even the birds in the trees have them on, Bob the buzzards maybe. Ha ha.'

'I feel really guilty, John. My poor mum has had to ask me for help because she is scared, and I didn't know she was scared because I had only seen them briefly when they returned from the Algarve and not for some time before that. Much longer than the two months they had spent abroad. Now, my dad is incapable of understanding my absence, and in a selfish way I'm relieved that he can't. He couldn't remember Mum's name when I saw him last.'

'I know, I heard. Your shot, mate.'

As a result of our dreadfully misguided second shots, we went our separate ways once more until reaching the green, when the separation ended, temporarily, obviously.

I said, 'I can't adequately describe how I feel, mate, but it has helped to say out loud what I've just said out loud. Thanks for being relatively quiet by your standards. Long enough for me to let me get it out loud anyway.'

'No problem. Three times you used loud there, you don't learn. Always here for you, Tiger. If Molly tells me anything that I think you might like to discuss with me going forward, I'll book another tee time.'

'Come on,' I said, 'let's see if we can find your ball in the rough.' (Before checking that he was carrying his spare bad-form ball.) My golf balls seem to prefer long grass and sand to the manicured fairway.

Mysteriously, John's golf balls change brand from Titleist, when they find the heavy rough, before re-emerging, rebranded, as a Ping, with no penalty points recorded on his card. The other John was right.

*

Back in the bar, after what a sports writer might describe as a sporting debacle – just a debacle really, nothing sporting about it, particularly when your opponent has cheated repeatedly, under the thin veil of competitiveness – we enjoyed beer and sandwiches.

'How is your dad, John?' I asked. 'Bill, isn't it?'

'No, I'm John, ha ha.'

'Seriously though.'

'Yeh, flat, mate, hard to tell with him. He's living alone with his memories and a really nasty Jack Russell, in a flat, mate. Like checkmate without chess pieces.

'He isn't, never was, wired to be in a close relationship. Not his fault. Whoever put him together got his wires crossed. My mum is Dad's second wife. The first marriage failed because of his social phobia and chronic, crippling depression.

'Mum once told me that Dad reaches a point when he feels he has nothing left to interest a partner, or to deserve another's love. He told me when I was round there last week that he was often lonely now, very often, actually, but he couldn't imagine having a "companion" in his life, let alone a partner, so he had to settle for loneliness. He hides it well from people he knows, though, and from me. Sam loves the bones of him and vice versa.

'He keeps his cards close to his chest, my dad, inside his chest, actually. Hidden, inaccessible.

'Before I left, head down, not looking at me, he said, "I can feel lonely, even when I'm in the arms of someone who loves me, son, when depression has me, as it does now. I'll battle on," he said. "Thanks for coming over, son. This might be the last of my many fights with my mind. I'm tired."

'Even roasties can't help him, Stevo.'

'Looks like we both needed a man chat, Johno.'

*

Bill awoke at 7 am the following morning after a restless night. Then went back to sleep until 9 am when he awoke again. He didn't want to stay in bed and he didn't want to get up.

After ten minutes of deciding what to do, he switched on the bedside lamp and groaned as he manoeuvred himself into a seated position on the edge of the bed.

There he sat, head down, shoulders dropped.

He was staring at somewhere between the carpet and his knees. His hands resting beside his legs. Bill would avoid studying his hands because they reflected his age right back at him. Liver spots, veins, painful movement, brittle nails and that leathery look, as he called it. Old man's hands.

A glance at his clothes lain on a cabinet led to the first physical challenge of his lonely day. He rose to his feet and stood awaiting confirmation that his poor balance and lightheadedness had been overcome on this occasion and that he would not be forced to return to sitting, before a second, sometimes third, attempt to rise successfully.

He dressed carefully and slowly, using the bed, a wall and a chair for support. Gone were the days when he could put on his trousers whilst standing, without some form of stabiliser. He shuffled into slippers, having stubbed his uncovered toes on so many occasions.

A wandering route to the bathroom and then into the lounge before sinking into an armchair, where he stayed, staring again, this time through French doors into the gardens behind his flat. He watched as other people went about their business. Jealous of their purpose.

He considered starting the tiresome process of assembling the cocktail of tablets that would control his blood pressure, heart rate and other conditions for the day. It could wait until he *had* to get up.

When his stare was interrupted, the television began dispensing visual medication of equal value to that prescribed by his GP.

Tinnitus had plagued him since he was seventeen. The result of standing too close to loudspeakers in a nightclub. Imagine, if you can, being able to hear two high-pitched whines, like old- fashioned kettles boiling in your head. Every second of every day.

The television provided some distraction and the radio stood in at night.

Bill would spend the day in the same chair. Unable to find the impetus to read or paint or write. His meals were borne out of convenience, not preference, and rarely required the cleaning of dinner plates.

Slowly, through the day, what little petrol he had in his will-to-live tank would burn off or leak away. So much so that if his son John rang and asked him how he was, Bill found it impossible to formulate a positive response in his mind and transfer it through the phone.

Friends who had previously attempted to prize him out of his flat had stopped visiting or phoning after many failed attempts.

The sadness he felt because of having no friends or company was killing him as surely, as slowly and as painfully as any cancer.

The phone rang. It was John.

'Dad. Can you hear me? There is no point sitting by yourself in the darkness. None.'

Bill thought how naive his son was with regard to depression. His message was simply code for, *Come on dad, pull yourself together*.

If only it was that easy.

Chapter 27

Driving home, I was thinking how much John knew about his dad, and how little I knew about mine. At the golf club, he had added that his dad was sixty-eight recently and that he had watched him age more quickly in the last six months than ever before. How he would have a Peter, Paul and Mary song on repeat in his flat because the chorus, although not a true reflection of the end of his relationships, made him feel guilty and he thinks he deserves to feel guilty. He knows of the pain he caused.

'Are you going away, with no word of farewell, will there be not a trace left behind?

Well, I could have loved you better, didn't mean to be unkind, you know that was the last thing on my mind.'

I asked my car radio to play the song and thought that the chorus might be what my mum was thinking, now my dad was going away. I put it on repeat.

'It's a lesson, too late for the learning.'

On the drive, I listened one last time – *'I could have loved you better, didn't mean to be unkind'* – before composing myself, and going in.

'Your mum's been on, hun. Can you ring her, please.'

*

'Hi, Mum. You okay?'

'I just wanted to thank you for yesterday, son. It doesn't feel like I'm on my own with it anymore.'

'No problem [they've got me doing it], I'll see you after work tomorrow. I'll text you my mobile number. Ring me at any time, day or night, promise?'

'I promise.'

'How is he?'

'He said earlier that he was fine. He's asleep again.'

*

'I'm nipping over to see Flatley tomorrow morning,' announced Dannielle, 'after I drop Martin off. I'll be back at midday. Allison has been on from work. They are looking forward to my return on the 24th.'

'Are you looking forward to it, Danners?' I asked.

'Sort of. Bit yes, bit no. Roast dinner with amazing roasties just craving to be microwaved and devoured when you fancy it, hun.'

'Do we have mint sauce?'

'Of course we have mint sauce. It's on the housewife's job description that you helpfully wrote out for me, along with brown sauce, obviously. What did your mum want? Is everything okay?'

'Not everything, but more things since I visited her on Friday.'

'And your dad?'

'Asleep.'

It struck me that I had said *'her'* not *'them'*. I had visited her not them in my mind. Subconsciously, I had separated them. They were now carer and patient, survivor and casualty, not Mum and Dad. From now on, I would ask, Hi, Mum. How is *he*?

I had two items on my to-do list. Dannielle's return to work was a big deal for her (and for me) after months of absence. Hats off to Allison for contacting her. I – or is it we – had a week to prepare Danny for take-off and I was at the helm, in Captain Kirk's seat. It was up to me to make sure that *all systems were go* beforehand and that Scotty kept my motor running. At warp speed if necessary.

Funny how I could have, quite correctly, used *it was down to me* instead of *it was up to me* and both would have the same meaning.

Chapter 28

'Have a nice week off, Steve?' asked Beth.

'Have you still got them?' asked her cohort, Lucy.

'Good to see you on time,' Beth said, quietly, pointing at her watch.

The lift maintenance guys had left, so she didn't feel the need to shout. 'Well, I didn't spoil Dannielle's birthday,' I revealed, 'and thereby I can confirm that yes, I do still have them.'

Lucy added, helpfully, 'The faint but distinct, lingering, unmistakeable, rather unpleasant smell of elephant still clings to you. I'm an observer of these things.'

'You don't observe smells, Lucy,' said Beth.

I (in no great detail) outlined the events of the 1st to the 7th of March. 'How has it been here?' was my way of saying I'm not taking questions on the subject.

'It has been hell here,' claimed Lucy, 'as we feared. We simply haven't been able to cope without you, O Mighty Oracle, have we, Bethy?'

'No, not because of a lack of effort, mind, on our part, more through a lack of ability or leadership.' (Hands to mouths, etc.)

'You're just like my eight-year-old sometimes, you two. Not growed up. And, by the way, I can't be O Mighty Oracle and Elephant Man at the same time. So na na nanna na.'

I admit that a combination of my return to work and thoughts about my dad reflected in my productivity that day. Our project manager, yet another normal John, doesn't miss a thing, and I will be questioned about today's performance, or lack of it, on my next appraisal. It struck me that I had definitive proof that one out of every three Johns is a cheat.

*

Danners had arrived safely at Flatley's home.

Edith, the lady who had been cast alongside Mona in the role of Flatley's dance partner, the beautiful and extremely talented Jean Butler, was in house, as they say.

Later, on her return home, Dannielle cast (clever that) some doubt on Edith's suitability. 'Well, she is heavier, slower, less coordinated, immensely less talented and unfortunately smellier than Jean Butler and had to be helped from the armchair she was nesting on before emptying her cup and leaving, shortly after my arrival. I said to my mum, "Mum, I thought they chose you because you looked more like a man than your fellow thespians."

'"That's what they told me," she replied, strangely flattered.

'"Whilst not wishing to be harsh or unfair about Edith, I am in no doubt, none whatsoever, actually, that she was offered the Flatley role before you and she must have turned it down. It must be of comfort to you that you are only the second-most manlike woman."

'Mum told me that fortunately for Edith she was impervious to criticism. Probably couldn't hear it actually. She had been Wishy-washy in the last Christmas pantomime, and not even that good, according to some. A fellow cast member, relegated to playing the back end of a cow, and briefly in a second role as a shining star in the sky, auditioned for the Wishy role, and that has to be taken into consideration when you hear that he was unflattering when describing Edith's costume as having the appearance of a flaccid air balloon.

'I also told her, "I couldn't help noticing that there was more tea on Edith's saucer than there was in her cup, Mum. Have you sold many tickets?"

'"Not exactly, but the show is well over three weeks off, well over, no need to panic yet, and tickets for our shows always go late, if they are going to go at all. Routinely, a high percentage of them marked as complimentary go to the nearby Candlelight old folks' home that specialises in the care of the deaf or hard of hearing. Many are returned. Those that do attend, some of them against their will, tend to clap in the wrong places."'

Chapter 29

'How long has he been asleep, Mum?'

'Too long for this time of the day but it gives me a break. He's started barking out tea orders when he is awake. No please or thank you, just tea.'

'I've been on Google, Mum. Apparently, dementia takes hold at differing paces varying from very slow to quick onset.'

'I hope it's the last one, son, for both our sakes. The blood tests have come back as I expected, Steve. The lady at the surgery has told me that a specialist dementia nurse named Sue will ring me tomorrow to arrange a home visit. The "in sickness and in health" thing keeps going through my mind, son. I lied. I fell out of love with your dad a long time ago, before all this started.'

'Mum, all sorts of thoughts must be going through your mind. You may want to keep some of it to yourself, but if you want to share some of it, or all of it, with your non-judgemental second- favourite son, I'm here. Soon you will settle on how to deal with this in your mind. Remember you are not alone.'

I sat with him for a while. Half of me wanted him to wake up, the other half didn't. He had no idea of the upset he was causing by being ill, and he would have been unable to process it, even if he was awake. As I watched him, I was trying to figure out, in percentage terms, how much I could give him, as opposed to Mum, Dannielle, Muffs and Snowy.

Mum was in the kitchen making me the panacea for everything: a nice cup of tea, with no sugar. There were tea stains on the front of Dad's pullover. He would have cleaned them off before all of this. I was comforted that he didn't know what the bloody hell was going on. I set up the sofa bed in the living room at Mum's request. Being next to him increased her feeling of separation. She wanted to sleep alone, upstairs.

What sort of disease is it that is capable of turning a respected, former senior mechanical engineer into a disoriented, detached, slobbering, wife-reliant adult in a matter of months?

I tried to imagine what messaging was going on between his eyes and his mind. His vocabulary consisted of two words. Tea and fine. There were thousands of words inside him that would never be used again. He had become a dictionary with all of its pages torn out.

There were no signs of emotion. None. No sadness or indication of feeling in his fixed expression. The subtle nuances in movement available to a healthy face had been filed away behind an unshaven mask.

Mum, wearing an apron inviting people to visit Torquay, returned with lovely tea and Rich Tea biscuits, which are the best dunkers. I hugged her, after she had put the tea and biscuits down (obviously; otherwise, all three of us would have had tea on our clothing). She needed it. She hugged me back, properly hugged me, like never before, longer than ever before. Until now, she hadn't been a hugger.

In a deliberate thought-through course of action, she had decided to care for *him,* not for her former husband, but for *him,* but only in the short term, she hoped, until someone was paid to care for *him.* She had detached herself emotionally from *him.* This was going to be a cold, functioning but dispassionate care home with one member of staff and one resident, and she was only prepared to work part time.

'Would you like me to be here for the home visit, Mum?'

'I would like you to be here as much as you can, son, but you have a family of your own and I want you to promise me that you will always put them first. Your father is an ex-person. Do you promise?'

I nodded.

'Okay. Good.'

I was a little surprised but relieved that Mum was able to mentally detach herself from Dad so clinically. I thought that some of the darkest days in a life that lay ahead of her would surely have been far more painful for her if her feelings for Dad had survived the passage of time.

*

The next day, specialist dementia nurse Sue was sitting in Mum's front room. I was there. Dad was awake but unaware. He had soiled himself. Sue spent an assessment period engaging Dad – no, trying to engage him – without success. She asked Mum how she was coping.

'*Coping* is the wrong word, dear. *Dealing* is closer. I don't know that person sitting opposite you, Sue, and I don't want him here. He is a stranger, a trespasser, with no manners, and I simply don't want him here. I repeat, I don't know him. I know you must think I'm horrible, but I don't know him.'

Sue caught my eye. She understood, I'm sure, unlike me, having seen it all before.

'I'm leaving shortly,' she said. 'Everyone reacts differently to the situation you find yourself in, through no fault of your own, Alice. Much of my time is spent supporting the partners, not the victims, of dementia. Some, including me, regard you, the carer, as the true victim because you understand what is happening. Promise me that you won't overanalyse how you feel. With respect, you are of an age when you know yourself and you must go with that. If you try to react the way other people think you should, you will betray yourself, doubt yourself, and drive yourself around the bend, and in doing so make dealing with this much more, far more, difficult, believe me. I will ring you on Monday. Your son and me are here for you. In that order. Lean on us.'

Sue (hugely impressive NHS Sue) had added herself to the team that would get Mum through this. In fact, she was the captain. When she left, Mum asked me if her own cold, selfish thoughts that she had revealed to Sue had disappointed me.

'No, Mum, I was thinking exactly the same. It would be difficult for you to hide your thoughts from anyone. Especially me.'

If I thought for one second that my dad knew where he was, or that he had understood our discussion, or that he knew he was unable to contribute and had no idea that two of the people in the room were his wife and son, I would regret him hearing our conversation with Sue. I thought to myself that you know when someone is struggling when you talk about him in negative terms whilst he is sitting next to you.

Instead, for the sake of my mum, and accepting that he was a passive, vacant attendee, I hoped that Sue would quickly find a bed in a care home where staff might medicate him sufficiently that he didn't experience whatever pre-death sadness he was hiding from us, if any.

I slept next to him on the couch that night, hoping to snatch a last ounce of awareness from him, a period – however brief – of lucidity that might allow him to understand that his son was right there with him, that he remembered my name.

As I watched his chest rise and fall, I knew that lucidity was thrown out with the pages of the dictionary, and I thought that life is unfair. It is very unfair. He and I endured a restless night. His body clock was showing the wrong time. No conception of light and dark. Just grey.

Chapter 30

'What have you been up to in school today, Marty?'

'Dad, why do you and Nanna Flatley call me Marty? No one else does.'

'Well, it's what I, and the former seven-times world Irish dancing champion's understudy, call a term of endearment, son. Our special word for you. Mummy has a special word for you when you won't get up for school of a morning, and lots of special words for me.'

'Could I use any of them in school?'

'Very few of them, mate.'

'What is Mummy's special word for me, Daddy?'

'Can't remember exactly, Martini, ha ha, but [dishonestly] it means Lazy Bones, broadly speaking. Where was I? Oh yeh, remember you call me Dad or Daddy depending on what you want from me, and no one else calls me that, as far as I know. Anyway, about today, spill the beans.'

'We didn't have any beans.'

'That wasn't what I meant, son, but it doesn't matter.'

'We did poetry, well, rhyming actually.'

'Obviously. What did you learn?'

'That the end of each line has to sound like the word on the end of the line above it. Otherwise, it's just writing. I prefer just writing because it's more quicker and you don't have to think as much.'

'What is the correct way of saying *more quicker*, son?'

'More faster?'

Close enough for now, I thought.

'Do you remember sitting on the sunbed next to me on holiday in Malta last year, Marty, when I was laughing at something that I was writing?'

'No.'

'Well, I was writing funny poems. I remember telling you. I've got two of them upstairs, folded inside my passport. Do you want to hear them?'

'No, thanks.'

'Tough, because you're going to.' I dashed upstairs to retrieve said poems.

'This one will make you laugh. It's called *Dressing*.

"I'm not the best at getting dressed, can't pull over my pullover.
I caught my toe in my underpants,
then what I'd describe as a pogo dance,
preceded a personal avalanche,
in slow motion, onto my bed
I lay for a while to recover, then I found one sock, not the other.
I pulled a fresh pair from a drawer,
of course they were inside out,
not something I'd normally quibble about,
but dressing was going so badly,
that I was starting to get real madly.
My trousers denied my feet entry, and the zip was as sharp as a knife,
it cut into my thumb, like a razor,
and has probably scarred me for life.
I have a hatred of hangers, and there they were all in a row.
I moved in a little bit closer,
and yes, you guessed, stubbed my toe.
So I'm hopping around, with no T-shirt on,
with blood on my thumb, going numb,
wearing socks that were obviously inside out,
and my underpants on back to front.
A second time, right on the Lego,
I fell on my bed, banged my head.
That's where I suffered the prolapse,
and kicked myself, in the Sunaks.

Now, there is no point getting angry,
don't want to be called a cross dresser. (clever, that)
In ending this poem, I confesser,
I prefer to walk round in the nude."

'How funny is that, mate?'
    'Helerus, Daddy.'
    'I think you mean hilarious, son?'
    'No, I mean Helerus, and some of the last words didn't match the
last words in the line above, so it's not even a poem.'
    'Okay, Mr Poet Laureate, try this one. It's called *My Travels*. I wrote
it for you, actually, out there, because you were only seven, and
irritating the life out of me because we weren't going to the water
park, ever again if I had my way. My back is still sore, and you weren't
doing enough reading. You must remember it?'
    'No.'
    'Standby for Operation Helerus. You too.' (Dannielle had joined us.)

'"I'm off to Kuala Lumpar, to meet an Oompa Loompa,
he feels the cold, I'm taking him, a string vest and a jumper.
And then I'm off to Bali, to meet with Charlie Farlie,
he's opened up a brewery and I'm taking him some barley.
A two-day trip to Venice, to see my old mate Dennis.
A naughty child at infants' school, in fact he was a menace.
A weekend break in Dover, to cuddle a police dog, Rover,
who'll follow me, in his marked police van, and ask me to pull
over.
Then I'm off to the Yorkshire Dales, where I'll buy a di-ary,
I'll make some notes, record some dates, and have buttered
scons with tea.
Next day I'm off to Brussels,
where Jane and John, the Russels,
will make me a Belgian paella.
Jane's very keen on muscles."

'This is my favourite verse, son. It is so good. Are you listening?

'"Then I'll shoot across to Palma,
to meet the Dalai Lama.

Together we will meditate,
he makes me feel dead calma.
My journey is almost over,
just two more stops to make.
I'm spending a day in Eccles,
where I'll make myself a cake."

"'Arriving back in Yorkshire, I saw my old friend Billy,
I'd been warm throughout my trip, I said,
but here it's really chilly."

'Nearly finished, Marty. Take your ear muffs off and listen, please.

"'So I popped into the tavern,
to buy myself a beer,
I do enjoy my travels,
but I much prefer it here."

'Ta-da. Round of applause, please, audience.'
'Daddy, did you spend too long in the sun out there,, and what is poet Larret?'
My listening, supportive, and I had hoped more appreciative, wife suggested – 'You should monetise that rare talent, hun. We could afford to get the kitchen done with our royalties. Most of the kitchen, anyway, well, a couple of cabine—'
'Enough, thank you. Firstly, they would be my royalties, actually, not ours. And secondly – you don't spend that much time in the kitchen, and [a drawn-out and, like aaannnddd] you haven't used the reasonably priced air fryer with very practical attachments and easy-to-follow instructions, yet. They're all still in the box, no doubt feeling impractical and unwanted, like me.'
'Ah, diddums.'

Chapter 31

The following morning, I left early for a breakfast meeting.

On Dannielle's return home from the school run, she was surprised to see two parcels on the lawn. (That wouldn't have surprised me.) When she stooped to pick them up, she noticed how perilously close they were to one of Snowy's free gifts, as it were, as if they had been aimed at 'it' like darts at a bullseye or bowls to a jack.

'That was lucky,' she said out loud.

Dismissing the deliberate notion as ridiculous and reasoning that their juxtaposition was entirely coincidental, she had a brief, confusing chat with old Ted next door before making her excuses. Just one blunt excuse, actually. Molly was en route for coffee and biscuits. Probably that oversensitive courier, she thought.

'Those parcels for Steve were lying on our front lawn when I got home, Molly. Aargh, and the old boy who lives next door has just asked me if Martin and Snowy enjoyed featuring in the *Jurassic Park* film that they and Steve were watching yesterday afternoon, and told me how he has told the lads at the domino masters tournament that he has two living film stars, actual living film stars, one a child and the other a dog, living right next door to him.

'Sad really. God knows where he got that from.' (Please don't tell her, God.)

'Well,' said Molly, 'I didn't expect those stories whilst driving here, Danners.'

*

At work, there was no sign of Lucy.

'Where's Lucy, Beth? It's very quiet without her.'

'She's under your desk.'

Now, you might have expected me to be surprised by that, even shocked, but despite having no idea *why* she was under my desk, I waited patiently for her to emerge before logging on. Even more unsurprising, I suppose, is that other than saying good morning to each other when she saw daylight, I didn't ask and she didn't tell.

'Well, how's my favourite anathema?' Beth asked me.

'Battling on, Beth,' I replied. 'I didn't think I would ever hear those two words riding the same tandem.'

From behind me and at – rather than under – her desk, I heard, 'What's an athama, Beth? My phone doesn't know what one is.'

'An anathema is a deaf cow, Luce, and an athama is a deaf calf.'

'Aargh, bit harsh, that, Stevo. No need for that, Bethany.'

Lucy worked flexi hours like Beth and left at around midday. I wondered, playfully, if she had gone to a potholing for beginners class and that her presence under my desk earlier was her way of preparing to be in a dark place below ground where only a nutter would journey alone and voluntarily. It might just explain the hard hat. I had considered working flexi in the past, but it would leave me vulnerable to more school runs.

It crossed my mind that workmates are rarely chosen. They are akin to family members. They are given to you. I remember working in an office where a small project team of only nine members was inhibited and eventually strangled by personal and professional differences. To be fair to the project manager, she addressed us on the subject of the group's discord and suggested that if cross- party motions were possible in Parliament then surely our group could put aside their differences in the interests of our own credibility and the company's interests. Despite an initial favourable response, she dissolved the group days later, deeming it beyond its purpose.

I was lucky to have Beth and the potholer beside me. We worked very well together in a spirit of respect for one another's opinion and experience. As a result, we achieved our purpose and enjoyed achieving it.

Chapter 32

On the school run-free journey home, I was watching a single engine aeroplane whilst stuck at the lights. Not in the next lane, you understand, in the sky. What kind of potholer thinks it's safe to get into something that small on your own and take off? My wingspan is bigger than the one above me, I thought. I have a sit-on lawn mower at home which sounds very similar but has a more powerful engine. It is in for repair, again, which reinforces the potholer theory.

The lights changed and as I travelled relatively safely on the ground, I was thinking about flying in general. I had read somewhere that the first people to pilot a plane that wouldn't fly were the Wrong brothers.

I don't like flying, it frightens me, and Dannielle is reliant on her trusted Valium/gin combo if she is to board one of those bigger ones. It makes her more irritable than usual. Hard to believe, but true.

The signs were there on a flight home from Faro to Leeds Bradford Airport, after our first holiday abroad together. She was conscious and breathing. That's all it takes, and likely to go off like a shower head does when you drop it in the bath whilst showering. She asked a flight attendant, in an irritated, drugged-up way, if she could change seats because of a crying baby next to her.

'I'm sorry, Madam,' the attendant replied, 'that crying baby next to you looks to be in his twenties or thereabouts, and you boarded with him so I can't help.'

'Reeaally, Dannielle,' I said, before joining the queue for a wee-wee.

Surprisingly, Martin, given his breeding, is not the least bit ruffled when in flight and would have made a good eagle. Despite his tender age, he senses our mid-air displeasure and does his best to comfort us. Since his seventh birthday, he has had an unhealthy interest in female flight attendants and their smart, tight, figure-hugging costumes, as he calls them. I don't know where he got that from, but he makes me very proud.

The tactic of shouting, 'What's that strange noise, Daddy, like something has come loose?' every ten minutes makes my journey a living hell and makes me fear a long-drawn-out, face-masked, overhead storage-emptying, dying hell.

Dannielle falls victim to his impressive knowledge of aeroplane crash statistics. Always useful when you want to terrify a passenger. Reassuringly, he reveals that – 'Mummy, no need to be afraid. We are safer, not completely safe, obviously, lots of parts on this one, but safe-er up here, Mummy, than on a train, on a boat or in a car driven by Aunty Molly. But [in a grandson-of-Peter-Cushing-type voice] when planes do crash, the casualty numbers are—'

'Enough, tell your Martin Cushing to be quiet, please, Steve,' she would say. Well, yell, plead actually.

Chapter 33

Next morning. 'Darling, have you ever been attracted to something or someone when you didn't know why?' I asked.

'I'm looking at a stark example of that right now, hun. Truth is, I still don't know why. What makes you ask?'

'Something I read in the paper yesterday at work. In the canteen, actually, to the left of the servery counter. Theory is that your subconscious is a far more dependable consort than your conscious on the grounds that the former has longer to think, and has far more life experience to rely on, than your conscious mind.'

'Don't know how to answer that straight away, Sigmund. Let me send an email to my subconscious,' Dannielle mocked, 'and see what comes back. In the message, after outlining the theory, I would ask...

Have you any idea why I am running with this question (because I don't) and do you have the answer? Please help. If you can't, please forward this email to my conscious mind on: Consious13@Danners.Com

Thank you for your experienced time. My conscious mind, a mere apprentice by comparison with you, will appreciate it.

Regards, Dannielle.

The *reply* read as follows.

Sorry I didn't get back to you on the meaning of life last week, Dannielle. I've been so busy. By way of apology, and in an attempt to answer your latest interesting, deeply relevant conscience/subconscious mind question, one that I have often wrestled with myself, at length, I have consulted two colleagues, both of them eminent psychologists, one of them fairly normal for one of those types, who share my view that it's a load of bollocks. I hope this helps.

Best wishes, always here for you both, regards, your sub.

PS I have taken the liberty of forwarding our stream to your conscious mind on the email address supplied, for a second opinion, or fourth opinion if you count the psychologists, actually...

You have new mail. Click.

Hello, Dannielle, how's it hangin'? I do hope that I find you and your subconscious well.

My thinking on this subject is typically knee-jerk, devoid of any lengthy thought process and based on very little experience when compared to your mighty subconscious (you may have detected the unmistakeable scent of sarcasm there), but despite that, I too feel that it's a load of bollocks. I hope this helps. I am bound by our ethical committee's rules to forward this stream to your GP – He or she may call you in for a chat ... Should call you in, actually, on reflection, not may call you in. I would. Stay reasonably well mentally and stop overthinking things. It is important that you consider my relationship with sub as an example of cerebral synergy, not a rivalry, and that you resist future dual contact that may fracture your states of mind by pitting one of us against the other.

Regards, etc.

The responses left Dannielle in two minds. (Clever, that.) Should she reveal that this had gone on inside her head, thereby confirming that she *was* indeed hearing voices, or should she simply give her head a wobble and press on, pretending she was normal? As if. She chose the latter, as opposed to the nutter I chose when we first met. Ha ha.

*

The afternoon became Father's Day without it being the correct date. I had planned to visit Mum to check how *he* was. John had invited his increasingly reclusive dad for lunch and Dannielle's mum had asked her to vet her dad for the third time ahead of a possible low money transfer from his flat to their former marital home. A return to his old club, if you like.

John's dad rang him to say that he didn't feel like leaving his flat that day and asked if John would visit him instead, which meant that all three visitors faced difficult away games. John's match was postponed after his dad rang a second time. John kept the reason to himself.

Dannielle's mum rang to prime her that she was, broadly speaking, in favour of the transfer. However, she wanted her dad to think it was in the balance, so that if selected to play, complacency would not set in within an hour of kick-off.

'I want him to think that there is a substitute on the bench, dear. A younger player, keen to impress if he was brought on. Fresh legs, if you will – leaner, stronger, firmer, more shapely, supple legs … Sorry, dear.'

'Will the sub be there when I arrive by any chance, out of interest?' asked Dannielle. 'He also needs a damn good vetting, don't you think?

My mum rang. 'Okay, I'm on my way. Twenty minutes tops.'

*

On arrival, he was on the floor, unable to get up. Mum was next to him, shaking. 'He fell just as I heard your car. Stood up, yelled tea, and fell, all in one movement, collapsed really.'

'Ambulance, please.'

Is the patient conscious and breathing?

'Not conscious, at least not fully, but he is breathing – in a very laboured sort of way.'

After a few more questions, I was told that an ambulance would be despatched as soon as one became available, probably within the next two hours. Suddenly the NHS crisis had slammed into my dad. It was 2.30 pm. I remember being told in a first aid class that the time of a collapse or a faint was important to the medics.

Collapse or faint, how bloody ridiculous; he had had, or was having, a stroke. The phrase 'every second counts' was looking back at me in the form of a helpless, vulnerable old man, with a bump on his forehead, above a face that had dropped on one side.

'Pass that pillow, please, Mum.'

'Is he all right, son? Shall I get him some Aspirin?'

A nice cup of tea was laid on the table next to me. The call handler rang back.

Is the patient conscious and breathing? she repeated.

'Yes, but he is struggling, really struggling. I think he's had a stroke. Can you get an ambulance here any quicker, please? Please. He is in a bad way.'

Do not give the patient any form of medication, and if he regains consciousness try to keep him talking. Stand by. Click.

Two minutes later, another click.

One of our crews has just freed up from a nearby hoax call. ETA to you, twelve minutes. Is there any change in the patient's condition?

'No.'

What sort of maniac makes a hoax call to 999?

'Mr Cunningham, I am Sue and this is Tom. We are both paramedics. May we come in.'

'Of course. Thank you for getting here so quickly.'

'Where is the patient?'

'He's in here on the floor. Please come in.'

'What time did he fall, do you know?' asked Tom.

'Two thirty on the dot.'

'That's really helpful,' said Sue.

'I was on the drive,' I said, 'when he fell, but Mum has said that he stood up and collapsed in the one movement.'

I asked, 'Do you want to go in the ambulance with him, Mum?'

'Mr Cunningham,' said Tom, shaking his head from side to side, 'we have to blue-light it to casualty, and with due respect, the combination of heavy braking, sirens, monitors and wires everywhere can be very unnerving for a passenger.'

'Okay, thanks for that, Tom.'

'Hi, darling. Dad is very poorly. A stroke, I think. Can you ask Molly to pick Martin up and then can you get over here to take Mum to the Royal. I'm going in the ambulance.'

'Are you okay, hun?'

'Yeh, I'm okay, thanks, but my dad isn't. See you in Casualty.'

*

'Dannielle will be here in twenty minutes, Mum. She'll take you. Try not to worry.' (What a stupid thing to say.)

The journey was exactly as described by Tom, possibly worse.

'How's he looking, Sue?' I asked, 'and please call me Steve.'

'There is no point insulting your intelligence, Steve. The patient is very poorly.'

'Will he make it?'

'I'm sorry, but that's a question for a doctor,' she replied. (Second stupid question.)

Sue's eyes met Tom's in the rear view mirror. Their exchange confirmed what she'd just told me about Dad's condition.

I was expecting a queue of ambulances but we went straight into a bay outside A&E. Inside, we were greeted by a team of gowned medics like one of the reception teams you see on *24 Hours in A&E*. Sue briefed the lead doctor and I was asked to wait outside the cubicle for a short period. Within minutes, he was on his way to a CAT scan. Travelling faster than you see on *24 Hours*.

'Are you a relative?' I was asked, politely.

'Son. Steve.'

'I'm Consultant Doctor Anne Atkins, lead clinician. The early signs are that your father has experienced what we call a haemorrhagic stroke.'

'A bleed to the brain.'

'A significant one. He is very, very poorly. So much so that I advise you to inform the appropriate people. Does he have a wife?'

'Yes. She should be here in around thirty minutes.'

'We will know more when he returns from the scan.'

'Thank you, Doctor, I'm very grateful.'

A second expression, passed between Sue's face and Tom's, confirmed my fears. Funny how watching can tell you more than listening sometimes, especially when you are in an environment such as this. I thanked them both for being paramedics, full stop, and for their help, before they departed, bound for another patient.

He returned some ten minutes later, in body but not in mind.

'Talk to him as if he can hear you,' advised a nurse. 'The truth is, we don't know whether or not he is capable of listening or understanding right now, but I would talk to my dad in these circumstances.'

Chapter 34

Doctor Atkins joined me in the visitors' waiting room.

'Mr Cunningham, I am very sorry to inform you that your father has, as I suspected, suffered a massive stroke.

'There is nothing we can do medically that might help him to recover from such an event. We will do all we can to make him as comfortable as possible, but my opinion is that your father will pass away sometime this afternoon. I can't be more specific than that. I'm sorry to bring you that very sad news. Do you have any questions?'

A shake of my head answered that particular question. She sounds quite cold and matter-of-fact when you read this, doesn't she. Quite the opposite was the case actually. She got it just right. I hoped I'd get it just right for my mum and Dannielle when they arrived. Later. I did.

He passed away with my mum and I holding his hands.

Before that, I spoke with, or perhaps *to*, him alone, in a closed curtained cubicle as he was slipping away. No one else around. All but one of the tubes had been taken from him. The only wires were those attached to a heart monitor.

His false teeth lay on a table beside him, the first time in ages that I had seen him without them, and the last time I would. Because of that, his face looked different somehow; smaller, older. So I put them back in his mouth, where they belonged.

'There you go, old man, you've got your choppers back. I recognise you now.' Unconscious, he was gasping for breath, gulping air, as if he thought he had a chance of survival. I remember thinking that my mum might miss his passing. Perhaps that would be appropriate. After all, she didn't know him.

Not sure.

'I hope you can hear me, old boy. I've come to apologise. I haven't been there for you, for far too long. As Mum said to me, I haven't exactly over visited, have I, and now it's too late. She will be here soon. Wait for her, if you want to.'

I continued. 'I deeply regret that because I hadn't "over visited", I didn't know that you were suffering until you were incapable of telling me or discussing it with me. What does that say about your son? Through no fault of your own, you weren't able to tell me if you were frightened, anxious, exhausted. The last time I hugged you, which was possibly the only time I have hugged you as an adult, you fell asleep, remember, on the couch. I really hope that you felt some comfort in my arms and that you knew it was me, your son, next to you. We never did much talking, did we. In fact, this is our best conversation in ages, although if you don't mind me saying, old boy, you're a bit quiet. I won't keep you much longer. Ha Ha.

'If the soul and the holy spirit do exist, I hope that yours have left the hospital and that they have gone ahead to prepare a welcoming party at wherever it is you're going. Goodbye, Dad. Safe journey. Love you.

'Don't worry about Mum. I'll look after her, better than I looked after you. I promise.'

Perhaps optimistically, I hoped that he was thinking, *Thanks, son. Love you too.*

Pessimistically, I didn't think he was listening. Standing beside him that day, I didn't feel guilt for some reason, nor did I cry. I knew, though, that at some time in the future, I would ... I did, and I do.

I bought a sandwich from the sandwich vending machine, a coffee from the coffee shop, and returned to the waiting room, to wait.

Chapter 35

What a day yesterday was. I had forecast a difficult set of away games, but not that difficult. I had woken up from an unsettled sleep to breakfast in bed with brown sauce, obviously.

'How are you, hun?'

'To be honest, darling, my thoughts are with my mum rather than me. I awoke to you this morning, and I love you so much, far more importantly than a full English with brown sauce.'

'Obviously. You old romantic, you.'

'Mum, however, has awoken to an empty house. If I lost you, I would be devastated, utterly, despite all the things you do that irritate me, and there are many. They are listed on paper in the top drawer of the bedside table if you wish to view them. I've done the same for Beth. That list is in a filing cabinet at work.'

I winked at Danners.

'Enough, Mr Perfect.'

*

'Hi, Mum. How are you?'

'Relieved, actually. I couldn't have taken much more of caring for that stranger. You think I'm horrible, don't you.'

'Not horrible exactly, Mum, but I worry that if I am diagnosed with a terminal illness that affects my mind, you might abandon me in the same way. Ha ha.'

'Abandon, is that how you see it?'

'I was only jo—'

'Abandon, eh?' Her voice iced over. 'There was a time when I would have done anything for that man, anything, I adored him. A time when I felt so proud of him and proud to be with him. A time when having you and your brother made me feel like the luckiest woman on the planet. Your father was earning an amazing salary, and spent much of it on me. I had everything I wanted, jewellery, everything. But – and it's a big but – slowly but very surely, I fell out of love with him. The man who died yesterday was not the man I married. I have kept it from you until now, and had intended to keep it from you forever until you said abandon.'

'Mum...'

'Abandon,' she repeated.

'I'll see you in twenty minutes, Mum. Get the kettle on, please.'

*

She continued from a chair that only yesterday had been his castle, his safety.

'When he retired, he changed. He missed being in senior management. He was no longer important to a team of professionals that respected him. No deadlines to meet. Instead, he was gardening and accompanying me to Morrisons, where the only decision he had to make was between carrots and parsnips. Often, sometimes in mid-argument, I would remind him that he was no longer the boss, that we were partners, not employees.

'Over a period of around five years, slowly at first, he became increasingly intolerable, impatient, patronising, insulting, selfish, condescending and horrible, frankly. We grew apart, and that suited me because eventually I disliked the man he had become. No, I hated the man he had become.

'So don't throw the bloody word abandon at me. I want to be alone. You don't know what the bloody hell you are talking about. If you had paid a greater interest in your parents' lives when he was alive, you may have bloody well picked up on it and protected me from him. He mistreated me, Stephen. Abandon? Please leave, before I throw you out.'

I left and took the long way home. In my head, it was raining, absolutely bloody bucketing it down.

So I drove back. She was crying.

'Come here, you,' I said.

I gave her a hug. She hugged me back.

'I'll put the kettle on, shall I,' I said.

Chapter 36

My mum was right. How had I allowed this to happen? I saw it, didn't recognise it for what it was, but ignored it. Too busy, not enough time. I had enough chances. Peter, Paul and Mary, popular, as you know, with John's dad, were on the radio.

'How many roads must a man walk down before you call him a man? How many seas must a white dove sail before she sleeps in the sand? How many times must the cannonballs fly before they are forever banned? The answer, my friend, is blowin' in the wind. The answer is blowin' in the wind.

'How many times can a man turn his head and pretend that he just doesn't see? How many times must a man look up before he can see the sky? The answer, my friend, is blowin' in the wind. The answer is blowin' in the wind.'

Dannielle had had an easier day. Despite her repeated attempts to bring on the substitute, her dad had signed an open-ended contract.

John's dad went to bed at 6 pm, again.

I had only met John's dad twice. The second time was at a small post-Christmas gathering a couple of years ago. He was very quiet, distant really. I tried to make polite conversation with him but his answers were closed. No, Yes, etc., and he seemed incapable of, or unwilling to catch my eye.

'Your dad's a bit quiet, mate.'

'That's the way he's been for a long time,' answered John. 'Well, before Mum passed. Occasionally, he can be quite "normal" but on most days he is like that. He takes anti-depressants, but they only seem to prevent him from going any lower rather than lifting him.'

I remember that Bill was the first to leave that evening. Unannounced at 5.30. He would have walked the solitary mile to his flat. Head down. Eyes glued to the pavement.

Part of him would have been relieved that he was no longer expected to socialise. Another part would have been wishing that he could, and that he was not walking alone, in the rain, towards an empty flat, where no one would welcome him. As usual.

'He'll be in bed by six,' said John.

He was.

Chapter 37

At breakfast – 'What has happened to Grandad Cunningham, Dad? Where is he?'

'Well, when grandads get very old and very tired and very unwell, they have a special sleep. One that they don't wake up from, mate. Your grandad has what we call died. We won't be seeing him anymore.'

'When did he died?'

'Yesterday, son.'

'Was he on his own?'

No, mate. Granny and Daddy were there with him. Holding his hands.'

'So, is he hurting?'

'No, mate,'

'Is he crying?'

'No, mate.'

'Where is he?'

'In a special room where died people go. Asleep. And his pains have gone.'

'So, is he on his own?'

'For now, son.'

'Why isn't Granny with him?'

'Well, she was, mate, but she needed to sleep and is in our spare bedroom.'

'Is she going to wake up, Daddy?'

'Definitely, mate. Granny is old but not very old. She is tired but not very tired.'

'Does she need a hug?'

'More than you would know, mate.'

'So, why didn't Grandad say goodbye to me?'

'Well, he wanted to, but whilst he was with me and Granny, he fell special asleep. He couldn't actually choose when it was going to happen.'

'So, will he miss me?'

'Absolutely. He asked me to frame a photograph he had kept of you, taken with you in his arms, soon after you were born. It was his favourite photograph. We could put it in your bedroom if you would like that, mate?'

'I would like that, a lot.'

Two, silent, beans on toast, with brown sauce, obviously, minutes later – 'So, will he stay asleep in the hospital forever and ever?'

'No, mate. He will be moved to a crematorium soon, where all of us will meet to remember him.'

'I don't have to go to a toriam to remember him, Daddy. So, will you and Mummy go to special sleep?'

'Yes, mate, but not for a long, long time, when you are growed up.'

'So, will I go to a special sleep?'

'Yes, mate, one day, but not for a long, long, long time. When you are a grandad.'

'Can you give Grandad a picture of me.'

'Yes, mate. No problem.'

'So, where will he go after the toriam? Did he tell you?'

'No, mate, he didn't know where he was going. It's a sort of a surprise.'

'Some people think they know where special sleep people go, but Daddy and I don't know. It's a nice place, though, mate,' said Mummy.

'So, naughty Phillip Reed told me that his grandad is died, and that he isn't there anymore when he goes around to his house anymore. Have we been to Grandad Cunningham's house, Daddy?'

'Not recently, mate, not recently.'

'So, okay, who's taking me to school? I need my PE kit, please.'

Chapter 38

At 7am, I lay awake in bed. My beautiful wife would look so peaceful and alluring, so feminine and delicate, even without makeup, if she wasn't whistling like a kettle. She can't whistle when she's awake. Funny that. It was unfair that I was thinking about her return to work and she was fast asleep in a whistle-making factory, in Whiston. Bit selfish that. She is hers, and so am I hers sometimes.

I was unsettled. The week would bring a very important deadline at work. I could do without it, with Dannielle's situation, the funeral and Cain playing up as usual on *Emmerdale*.

If Martin had knocked on our bedroom door, I would have invited him in and stolen his headphones from his flat-eared head.

At breakfast, as I sat chain yawning, she breezed into the kitchen after a 'lovely sleep'. The physio uniform that had hung in the wardrobe for months suited her. She looked good, really good, sexy, professional. My naughty side slipped, like an avalanche in the Northern Alps, if I'm honest, towards a role-play scenario. Sorry, sorry.

'What are you thinking about, hun?'

'Oh, you know, this and that, darling. [Mostly that actually.] Are you ready for it, darling?' (A blatant double entendre.)

'I feel quite excited actually, really ready for it.'

'I'd hoped you might say that, darling.'

We had lapsed on *that* front in view of recent events and I was looking forward to some scrotal recall, with her in that uniform, definitely, name badge, upside-down watch, the lot, for about ten seconds anyway. Tops.

I was keen for her to know that me, Martin and to some degree Snowy were proud of her. Martin gave her the *good luck* card we had made secretly, and that turned on her facial taps. Unable to find her stop tap, she read our messages out loud.

Snowy's was a typically understated but nonetheless sincere paw print.

Martin wrote, *To the bestest mum in the world Gud luck. xx*

Knowing that Martin would read my message, I steered away from the uniform thing, for now at least, and went with:

So proud of you, darling. xxx

I had beaten Muffs on the x front and that made me happy.

Danny was rota'd to work part time, Monday to Wednesday, 10 till 2 for the first week to ease her back, and other people's backs hopefully, so she was doing the school run. Two wholly sloppy, rather drooly, snotty, whiskery kisses later, which Snowy and I were grateful for, and she was on her way.

That very smooth, poor-hygiene start to Dannielle's day was a huge relief for me, and my thoughts turned towards work.

My car was in the garage so I travelled in by taxi. The driver, who was an overtalkative but pleasant enough type, revealed that, like me, he used to work under pressure in an office. But no more, he said 'I'm my own boss now. I work when I want to, and when I don't want to, I don't. Nobody tells me what to do anymore. And I love it.'

'Next left,' I told him.

Chapter 39

Breaking news arrived by mail in the form of a circular entitled:

Padside Players – Is it the end this time?

Due to a total lack of interest, less than that, actually, in ticket sales and the one hundred percent return of the complimentarys from the Candlelight care home, core supporters hitherto, Flatley and Brown had been stood down.

In an unnecessarily blunt and demoralising but sincere letter from the care home manager, a Mrs Anne Thompson RN BSN NASTY (hons.) wrote that it is an important, ongoing part of their care regime to seek ways of lifting the spirits of their residents, some of whom are battling anxiety, boredom and depression. If the Padsite's last Christmas panto was anything to go by, it would just make things worse for them if they were to attend the 'Riverdance Experience', or 'pond dance' as mischievous Gladys Philpot has prophesised will be more descriptive. Another Gladys (they have three) had told their staff nurse that news of the cancellation had lifted her suicidal thoughts significantly, like no medication before it, to the point where she had stopped planning her funeral.

Mrs Thompson went on, and on, to say that she sensed that there were other (hardly detectable if you didn't know the residents individually) indications from most, in fact, I can't hide it from you, why should I, for goodness' sake, *all* forty-two residents, actually, that even a very poor episode of *EastEnders* would be more endurable. Phyllis Darby, now the late Phyllis Darby, commented that at least they could turn that off.

Old Alf had rudely, but in character, expressed the view that he would rather watch a play about incontinence. *I might add that Alf is a true expert, a gifted exponent in the field and anywhere else where he happens to be standing.* He was proud of his nickname, Flash Flood, telling both of his fans that he should be classed as intercontinental because he had also wet the bed in Asia and Africa, and would have in Antarctica, given half a chance, if he had visited there.

Mrs Thomson finished, finally, with – *I would like to end on a more positive note but I can't. Other than perhaps to inform you that (our third) Gladys' sprained ankle is improving rather nicely.*

Fond regards, etc.

PS If you feel the urge to forward tickets in the future, fight it.

Now, fair play to the Players to circulate this unsolicited, nasty pre-performance critique. They could have blamed COVID. The document finished with an invitation, no, an appeal, a bordering-on- desperation kind of appeal for new members, cleverly enticing them in by a promise to have the chair lift working soon, if not sooner, and a commitment that the banister, which had proven invaluable, indeed lifesaving, on so many occasions, will be screwed back onto the wall as soon as the rawl plugs are budgeted for.

Clearly, they had brought in a marketing genius who had had the foresight to include that those with acting experience are not only welcome but will be treated like thespian gods, pedestal dwellers. Furthermore, with talent retention in mind, an unprecedented 'actor of the year' accolade will see the crowning, every twelve months, of our greatest crowd puller.

Applicants without acting experience will not, will definitely not, let me be very clear about that, not be invited to join us because we have enough of them in our ranks already, and those rejected are advised to take up another art which does not require talent or aptitude or include the threat of an audience ... however small in number, press ganged, unimpressed or hard of hearing those watching may be.

The local paper were invited to headline the dilemma and the search for help. The editor revealed that a literary source, an insider no less, had informed him that a pathetic, embarrassing letter, desperate in tone, delivered to and binned on receipt by Bill Nighy's people, was an indicator of an endemic lack of anything closely bearing a correct course of action amongst the group's top executives.

In closing, he confirmed that he was unable to help, not prepared to help, actually, and that any mention of the Padside Players, even carefully hidden on page 9, near to the caravan sales, would be contrary to the paper's mantra of bringing the often stark reality of life in North Yorkshire to its readers and occasionally some fairly interesting news.

'Hi, Mum.' Danny phoned. 'Sorry to hear about the appalling lack of interest in you, not you, sorry, *the Experience*.'

'I'm not surprised, dear. I wouldn't have gone myself if I wasn't in it, starring in it, actually.'

'Why didn't you ring me rather than sending the pamphlet?' Danny asked.

'Well, for accuracy, it is a circular, dear, not a pamphlet.' She continued. 'I landed on my glasses again yesterday and an arm has fallen off, not my arm obviously. So I couldn't have read it to you on the phone.'

'I see.'

'Don't start that again, dear. I was doing the Flatley teapot thing with a straight-armed spout when I lost my balance again and landed, just like the previous time, on my glasses, on the couch.'

That smalltown Piers Morgan and Hattie bedpan Jacques from the home went over the top, don't you think?'

'Not really, dear. I had an inkling the newspaper wouldn't help us, because I am the source he has referred to. The insider.'

'How is Jean Brown?'

'Disappointed, naturally. She told me that she felt good in her air balloon costume, that she felt beige suited her, and that she was flattered by the comments from whoever was in the back end of the black and white cow. She hadn't recognised the voice because it was so muffled. She also heard both ends of the brown cow giggling, apparently. I think it would have been the first time that she didn't have to learn any lines and would therefore be able to put every stone of her stage presence into mesmerising effect. In our last play, she played a mother who was playing hide and seek with her daughter. She only managed to reach four before the prompter was called upon to help her up to ten.'

'Mum, without wishing to sound cruel, but being unable to avoid it, how on earth was she chosen for a lead role? She makes Benny from *Crossroads* look like a Golden Globe nominee.

'Now, how can I put this without offending your delicate nature, Mother? Is she making the casting man's roast dinners, if you get my drift?'

'No, dear, and I do get your drift. His sprouts are steamed, if you get *my* drift, by the local blacksmith. A rather muscular, broad-shouldered, handsome, tight white tee-shirt-wearing, furnace-glowing chap who, God willing, is bisexual.'

'Mother!!!!'

'Sorry, dear, sorry.'

'Anyway, on a completely different subject, the antithesis in truth, the reason why I'm ringing *was* to make sure you were okay, but that has changed, only a minute ago, actually, to arranging a convenient day next week to visit. Quite possibly every day next week.

'Out of interest, Mum, no more than that, can you see the sprout steamer from your living room, per chance?'

'Ohhhhhhh yes, dear, but you have to stand on the couch.'

Chapter 40

'**M**ate,' said John via telephone, 'Molly wants me out of the way for a coffee morning on Saturday. By the way, she has somehow found out that a car driven by her is said to be on the list of most perilous journeys.

'If I find out who said that, I will add aviation fuel to the fire by mentioning that I refuse to be in the same car with Stirling Molly if there is a steering wheel in front of her.

'Truth is, my dad is not at his best, mate, far from it, and I would be grateful for a man chat. Apologies, I know it's raw given your dad's departure but, I admit, I don't know how to deal with it. Can we meet at the driving range at about ten? Yep, no problem. See you there.'

*

The funeral was functional and procedural; no more than that. The poor attendance backed up my mum's view that he wasn't the best company in his later years. Martin, attending his first funeral, decided to remain silent throughout, other than to answer yes, on the numerous occasions when his mum or I asked him if he was okay, and squeezed his hand.

The only words he uttered were 'Did Grandad get my photograph, Daddy?'

'He did, mate.'

What Marty didn't know was that a rare photograph, taken of him with his grandad, in fact one of only two of them photographed together, lay next to my dad as he left by conveyer belt. The other photo was framed, and on the wall in Muff's bedroom.

In the lobby, we were asked to move on because *the next one* was about to start. The wake was also poorly attended, and the amount of buffet food left over told its own story.

I don't believe that he was watching over us, some do, but if he was, it struck me that he may be regretting becoming an irritable, selfish, self-opinionated, ungrateful old man in later life.

It felt wrong to ask if I could take home a doggy bag. Perhaps the thing that upset me most was that a huge bowl of coleslaw went undoggy bagged, and I had paid for it.

Mum was okay. That was the most important thing for me. She smiled politely when the few that did attend expressed the obligatory lovely man opinion. She wasn't just biting her lip when they did; she was chewing on it.

'Tell me, son,' she asked, 'how can twenty minutes in a crematorium be a respectful, fitting end to seventy-four years of life?'

Marty went to bed at 7.30 and hasn't mentioned his grandad since.

So a week that brought me deadline pressure at work, my dad's funeral, Danny's return to work and industrial-scale coleslaw wastage, drew to a close. Not forgetting that John had asked for my help on Saturday, which is, technically, part of a week.

I regard John as my best mate, but after such a week, his timing, predictably, was poor. Or maybe it was his dad's timing that was poor.

A Friday night followed which was dedicated exclusively to Danners, Muffs, Snowy and me. We all put on our most comfortable, baggy clothes, sat on the couch together, close together, and enjoyed red wine and a takeaway pizza. 'I love you three so much,' I told the three beings present.

'That red is a bit dry for me, how about you three?' asked junior. He got that from his mother. Snowy was asleep and twitching, the way he and Dannielle do during slumber. At least Snowy doesn't whistle in his sleep.

The snow man didn't answer the wine question, but it was very nice of Marty to include him.

Later, whilst falling asleep, with Dannielle and, surprisingly, Snowy in my arms, I hoped that after helping John with his dad problem, I would experience a long, long, uninterrupted, well-earned period of family, enjoying golf playing; birdie scoring; expedition-filled, problem-free, wife and son treating; Snowy walking; coleslaw devouring; match watching; wine buying; decorating-free, alcohol-fuelled break from life's challenges. Good night, Sleeping Beauty, and good night, Dannielle. Ha ha.

Chapter 41

Zero six thirty hours, me, Snowers, wearing his new collar, on the path that runs along the edge of the canal. A bright, crisp early spring morning as a jogger running towards me on the path that runs along the edge of the canal wished me good day. Well, sort of.

She asked, breathlessly, 'Does your dog bite?'

'Of course, but not people.'

Snowy's friend, a lady dog named Missie, with a lovely nature, was up ahead and Snowy ran on, quickly, too quickly, to greet her. I had warned the snow man about wearing his heart on his paw, but to no avail, obviously.

I imagined him telling his bitch, in Labrador that his collar was too tight, that he was surprised that his head was still on and that it was a new present.

Oh, I love it, darling. Although your eyes are a bit bulgey. I imagined she would bark in Poodle.

Snowy really enjoyed her company. She was, after all, single, pretty, obedient (risky) and house-trained. What more could a man want? He had let himself down when they first met (in the eyes of some dog owners) and had to be loudly admonished, publicly penalised, when his hot bitch was in season. I remember, 'Snowy, No! Sorry about that. Come here *Now,* Snowy! Sit!' As a ruffled but clearly smiling Missie was led off to two weeks in isolation, and as soon as it was safe to do so, I stroked Casanova's head. 'Good lad, Snow Man, good lad. Good to know that you know how things work.'

For a peaceful, tranquil, birdsong mile, we walked together, alone, a man and his dog, facing life full-on, on a path. In a field behind a fence that ran alongside the path that ran, etc., a rarely seen March hare was pruning itself. Must have good hearing with those bad boys on its head, I thought. Only a few days ago, it would have been a February hare.

Then, emerging from the distant, haunting and mildly polluted early-morning mist, the unmistakable throaty roar of a long boat engine as it tore through the slowpids and powered towards us at well over three knots, well over, causing tiny wake-like ripples that slammed into the canalside bank, that runs alongside, etc. No surprise that joggers and dog walkers flocked here. I'm told that canal boating is the fastest way to slow down. I like that. The customary wave from a flat-capped, pipe-smoking pilot completed the scene.

In the next field, a small herd of alpacas, or were they llamas? Like the one with two heads in the *Doctor Doolittle* film, but with one less head and one more tail. Just one tail each, actually. Snow Man was part cautious, part curious, and part petrified within their proximity, so as a precaution, he would leg it until he could no longer see or smell them.

Word was that one of their number – a flaming red looker of a llama, named Smokey – had been taught to detect smoke and fire, and was advertised on a billboard in the local village store as being for sale, as a fire alama. I like that.

Llamas, as you know, are often mistaken for alpacas. By sheer coincidence, that same day, an Italian couple who live next door to the local village store where Smokey was advertised for sale, Al and Paccalina Vicenti, were planning to ramble.

Al, a keen backpacker, asked Paccalina, 'Alpaca a picka-a-nicka basketa, shalla, Paca?'

'Sì, Al,' said Paca.

Priceless that, reader; you can't teach it.

Cattle, however, although much larger, didn't seem to bother Snowy. I could imagine him facing down a fearless black and white one (without actors inside it) from a safe distance and goading it with, 'Come over here and moo that if you think you're hard enough, Johnny Beefy Boy Concrete.

'But I must warn you,' he would add defensively, 'that luckily for you beefers, that two-metre- high, impregnable, reinforced metal fence that runs between us is very heavily and very dangerously electrified. Not to mention the canal and whatever lurks hidden and menacing beneath it between your bank and mine.'

I was safe with such a fearless, though rightly cautious, companion whilst out walking, unless, of course, we were walking, or probably running, or legging it in truth, in an impregnably fenced field, with a herd of black and white beasts behind us, led by their toughest, meanest, surprisingly fleet-footed, feared champion bull, Johnny Beefy Boy Concrete.

Chapter 42

'Coffee first, mate?' I asked John.

'Yes, please, mate.'

'Sorry about your dad, mate. Lovely man, I hear.'

'Thanks. What's happening with yours? I am guessing that you haven't shared your thoughts with Molly, not deliberately anyway, or Dannielle would have told me ...'

'No,' he replied, aware of that danger.

'Be careful around Mollers, John, she *can* read thoughts from five metres. How is she? Haven't seen her in ages.'

'She's good. Look, I know you could do without this after your week, Steve ...'

'But?'

'Yeh,' John continued, 'but he is closing down in front of me. I can see it and I feel helpless. I was round at his yesterday and some of the things he said have been giving my ability to understand him a good kicking.'

Experience had taught *me* to remain silent at times like this. I was here to listen, not to talk (too much).

'I was with my dad for at least ten minutes before he asked me why I had been in touch with him so much lately.

'"You're either more stupid than you look, Dad," I said to him, "or you must realise I'm checking on you, and please, don't say why. You know why. You're doing your disappearing act again, aren't you, deliberately. Thinking back, you've done this before, often, more often the more I think about it, but you are making a better job of it this time."

"'I don't want to discuss it, son," he said. "It's private and very, very hard for anyone who hasn't lived with chronic anxiety and depression to understand. Bloody debilitating, unable to shake off anxiety and depression, I don't want to be like this. It has crippled me throughout my life and still does.'"

John asked me, 'You might be wondering how I am remembering all this, Steve. I don't think I have ever listened harder in my life, that's how. Pass the sugar, please.' John was choosing eye contact with his coffee rather than with me.

'Do you know, and you may not believe this, he was first prescribed tablets for anxiety when he was just fourteen, and has been on some form of medication for *sixty years,* and yet I never once saw him take tablets that weren't just painkillers!

'Anyway, Steve, having said he didn't want to discuss it, my dad continued. "Your mum, who shared and suffered my depression with me, God bless her, had no choice other than to leave me. Or did I leave her? I can't remember. She was always worried sick that you might inherit my nightmare, so she banned the words anxiety and depression from your ears, and the sight of it in any form from your eyes, in case it triggered something inside you.

"'What might I have been like if my life had been medication-free, son? Too late now, I am an addict. If I forget to take my tablets, I know within a couple of hours because of an all-consuming, physical, not mental, tent-over-a-dead-body sensation which I find impossible to describe accurately. The word sensation is wrong, actually, because it sounds like a good feeling. It's a terrible feeling, and whatever the correct word is, it grips you like the hands of a rock climber, and then the hands slip from the rock.

"'Son, I have said all I am going to say, all I can say, for now at least. More than I have ever said to anyone, other than to psychiatrists or my GP, Dr Tseung, who has been in my passenger seat over the last twenty years, who has refastened my safety belt for me when I wanted to jump out. If you ever want to thank a member of the NHS for my survival, he's your man.

"'Good night, son. It's nearly 6 pm. Time I was in bed.'"

John's head was in his hands.

'Sorry, mate, can I have a few moments alone, please?'

'Of course. Cornish pasty with red sauce for two coming up. I'll sit over there by the window. Join me when you're ready, or if you prefer, get into your car and leave if you wish. I will understand. I'll eat both pasties, no problem.' I patted his Popeye-sized forearm and got to my feet.

I was hiding my own emotions, which were not exactly overflowing, but they were letting me know that they were there nonetheless. Do you know, I actually envied John. He had set up and taken the chance to speak to his dad about 'it', and I suspect that his dad, despite the prompting, was grateful for an opportunity to talk about 'it', however reluctantly, initially. He and John may share a second phase of discovery and revelation in the coming weeks. Something I can't do.

'I'm ready for this pasty, mate.'

John, who had swopped his coffee for my eyes, patted my Olive Oyl-sized (by comparison) forearm and said, 'Grateful, mate.'

We exchanged barely perceivable nods of our heads, and moved on to the most discussed golfing conundrum known to man or woman, particularly golfers. What *is* the best way to grip a putter? One of life's great mysteries, well, certainly one of golf's. One that punches you in the face if you don't know the answer, and then in the stomach, when you three put on the eighteenth before throwing the damn thing in the brook.

*

'How did it go at the pointless, time-consuming, hitting-a-little-ball-at-a-flag-with-a-stick party, hun?' asked Dannielle on my return.

Chapter 43

My brother, Phillip Cunningham, now an Australian citizen, was backpacking around New Zealand, apparently. The telephone number Mum has for him was answered by his housemate, Zac, who revealed that he had not heard from 'Cunny' for some time and that, true to form, he had not been left with any way of contacting him. As a result, my brother was unaware of his dad's departure, a week on from his death. Zac was asked to pass on the news to the travelling prodigal when he returned.

'Do you think he's all right, son? I do miss him.'

'No idea, Mum, not concerned. I do wonder sometimes how he finances these absences, when he wanders abroad, so to speak, as he often does, preferring the state of isolation and solitude that leaving your mobile with your mate brings. Sir Francis Drake used to do something similar, apparently, but he took gallons of rum and eighty sailors with him. His mum could never get hold of him.

'Of course, it's not true isolation, Mum, because he left his phone and charger in the hands of someone he knows, who he could call on another phone, probably the SIM-only one in his rucksack, if he found himself in a state of needing assistance. Probably in a state of money-needing assistance. Hardly Christopher Columbus, is he, Mum? Terrapin Dundee perhaps. And you can be sure that he will ring you about Dad's will as soon as he breaks cover, when the dingoes are sleeping. Did you and Dad ever figure out why he is a foot smaller than me?'

'Can you ever see a time when you and your brother might patch things up, son?'

'No.'

'Oh, and Stephen, I wonder if you could find time to help me with your dad's stuff. There must be some things in the loft as well that I can't get to. I think he must have a secret train set, he was up there so often.'

'Of course, Mum. I'll send Sniffer Snowy up first to locate the heroin stock, and then I'll meet up with the Fat Controller.'

Chapter 44

'I have no illusions about the future, Beth. Our success in reducing the company water bills by 0.63 per cent has left us vulnerable to instructions, one might say commissions, from people like Derek "Lecky" Davis, who heads up electrical things, and Harriet from heating, who, I have to say, can be very cold sometimes, don't you think?'

'I do,' said Beth, warmly. 'I worked with "Icy Blast", as she's known, last year, and wore an extra layer when she was around. I thought that round of applause we received in the canteen earlier was much deserved, hard earned, nice, though, didn't you?'

'I did, although I think technically, Beth, to be properly described as a round of applause, it requires there to be more than three clappers, preferably many more, in a theatre if possible. Otherwise, it's just a clap.

'John from the pay department, he's so funny, isn't he, that John? Creases me sometimes,' I said, 'has emailed me claiming that following a detailed study, he has found the secret to eliminating staple wastage.'

'I have had a similarly hilarious one in the same vein,' said Beth, 'from Sally in marketing, who suggests, helpfully, that we would save upwards of a very small fortune if we brought in new rules around Sellotape usage. If staff were instructed to stick to them, the rewards would be substantial, with the added bonus that packages would reach their destination intact. True genius right there.'

'It's tough at the top, Beth. Get used to it, enjoy it, look down on people, be aloof, practise arrogance, be your normal self, in fact, because it won't last forever. There is always an irritating subordinate waiting in the shadows, desperate for a clap in the canteen or anywhere else. I've seen it in the Tavern.'

'How dare you talk to me about arrogance. In fact, how dare you dare to talk to me at all,' said Beth, smiling with that arrogant look she has, and looking down on me.

*

My mum rang that evening. The story goes that to Zac's great surprise he had been contacted by my brother, Phillip, using a fully charged mobile borrowed from another man of the wilderness, about an hour after he received Mum's call. Now, the most cynical would call that utter bollocks. The less cynical would agree, and the good people of St Swithin's Church would claim that the Good Lord and his happy band of telephonists act in mysterious ways.

'He didn't sound upset at the news, Stephen, and didn't ask how I am, or how you are. It seems that within the hour between me speaking to Zac and Phillip ringing me, he had read on Google that in such circumstances, a letter of agreement in the form of an affidavit would allow the will stuff to go ahead in his absence. He told me that he had our, now my, home address and would forward the letter immediately. He added, "It will arrive within four to six days."'

Perhaps cynically, I had a mental picture of a rucksack, with a laptop and power cable inside, nestling next to a SIM-only mobile phone, in the house he shared with Zac. If that was his real name.

Chapter 45

'Are you sure you want to throw everything out, Mum?'

'Every last bit of it, son, except perhaps the train set, which Martin might like, if there is one up there. Or you might like, you big baby. I'll take any decent clothing to the charity shop. Dannielle has told me that you still prefer *Teletubbies* to *Coronation Street*. I can imagine you as Tinky Winky.'

'Thanks for that, Mummy. Only thing is that Ringo Starr's voice irritates the life out of me. He sounds so disinterested. So no sound, please.

'Is there one of those folding ladders up to the loft, Mum?'

'There is; otherwise, Chris Bonington wouldn't have progressed beyond base camp. Mind your head. Your dad often came down to earth with a bump and a self-diagnosis midway between bruising and concussion. Unknown to him, I have nicknamed the ladder "Grace" because he has often fallen from it.'

'Heeyyy. Clever that, Mum. I can see where I get my sense of humour from now. I'm a little nervous of what I might find up there, to be honest.'

'So am I, son.'

A Blu-Tacked *Keep Out* sign on the landing ceiling was a warning.

'He was probably only joking with the sign, Mum.'

'Your dad didn't joke, son,' she replied.

'Mum, I'd assumed that there would be a light switch near to the trapdoor but I can't find one. Do you have a torch?'

'We used to have one in the cutlery drawer, but it went missing after the *Keep Out* sign was posted.'

'Well, Mother, unless you can persuade the roof tile-penetrating, 2000-lumens North Yorkshire Police helicopter to assist, I will have to return on another day with a torch.'

'Shall I ring the helicopter people and see if they are busy at the moment, and able to help?' she asked.

I wasn't sure if she was being serious. That's probably where I get that from as well.

*

The following day, by appointment, I resembled a clean-faced miner as I nervously, rung by rung, climbed the reasonably priced, folding light aluminium stairs to the entrance of Aladdin's cave. I could hear the theme tune from *Jaws*, although, as far as I know, Jaws lived in the sea and was never in dry dock, in a cockloft. Within seconds, I had located the light switch that had eluded, and not illuminated me, the day before. More like one of those huge levers that railway signalmen pull in a signal box than a switch, but I had missed it. Easily done in the dark. A contradiction in terms if ever I heard one.

No train set. Almost no anything, but for a two-piece, roughly four-feet-square boarded area, a stool, a torch and a small cardboard box that you could fit a toaster in. That was it. My miner's headlamp scoured the roof space in search of something that might command a good price on the *Antiques Roadshow*, but only an intrepid insulation enthusiast would risk a journey beneath the slates. Let's be honest, if you picked up a paperback entitled *Journey Beneath the Slates (a beginner's guide to the fascinating world of cocklofts)*, by someone whose name was Norris Brown, you would put it back down, like it was a stinging nettle, on the unread second-hand book sales shelf.

'Is there much up there, Stephen?'

'No, Mum, just a small box, and a stool.'

'How odd,' she said. 'Before we went to the Algarve, he was always up there, no doubt on that stool. Let me guess. Is it one of those three-legged tatty-red-seat kind of stools?'

'It is, yes.'

'I wondered where that'd gone. It used to live in the shed. Like your dad a lot of the time.'

I retrieved the box, turned off the light, extinguished my headlamp, closed the loft hatch and removed the *Keep Out* sign before joining Mum in the kitchen.

'I'll just wash my hands, Mum, it's a bit dusty up there. Back in a minute.'

On my return, I found the contents of the box laid out like court exhibits on the kitchen table.

'The stamps on those letters have kangaroos on them, Stephen.'

'Really? Have you ever seen them before, Mum?'

'Of course, that's how I recognised them.'

'The letters, Mum, not the kangaroos, Michelle Attenborough.'

'No, I've never seen them. Your dad would get up before me in the mornings and insisted on being head of letters. Every so often, he would greet our postman on three, sometimes four, consecutive days, one after the other for some reason. I know that because their blurred conversations in the vestibule below my room used to wake me up. Very odd. But then again,' she added, 'he was studying Odd with the Open University, and was doing very well, apparently.'

There were eight travel-weary envelopes, all in the same hand, all addressed to my father, as well as a notebook, a pocket diary dated 2020, a pack of unused envelopes, a few stamps without kangaroos on them and two pens. I put them all back in the box and returned home, intrigued and in search of my reading glasses. A gesture from a pedestrian, which I initially read as a criticism of my driving, and at the same traffic lights that gave life to Chapter 27, led to the removal of the headlamp that had explored Dad's cave earlier.

'Are you a potholer?' the pedestrian asked.

'Sometimes,' I replied.

*

Meanwhile, Danny and Molly were enjoying an overdue coffee morning in their favourite teashop in the bustling village of Ingleton. My terminus, you may remember, at the end of that day in North Yorkshire.

One point nine miles east of Horton in Ribblesdale, in the shadow of the mighty aforementioned Pen-y-ghent. Where the River Doe and the River Twiss join to form the River Greta, a tributary of the River

Wenning, and eventually the River Lune. I hope that information is helpful to you when visualising their location, dear reader.

Some important issues like my dad's death and John's dad's battle with depression were overlooked, nay brushed aside (except one), in favour of Dannielle's frustration at not yet having had the opportunity to show off her Jimmy Choos, and Molly's elation (after swopping from the toe- breaking world of kick boxing to karate) at her award of the coveted white belt.

Dannielle was suitably impressed, obviously, but blissfully unaware (luckily for Molly) that the more-difficult-to-attain orange, blue, yellow, brown and black ones, unmentioned by the warrior queen opposite, require a little more mastery than just punching the air repeatedly and yelling *Huu* with no socks on. There was one, very important, very delicate, topic of conversation Molly had left until after they had eaten their scones.

Chapter 46

'Molly is four months pregnant. It's a girl.'

I gave up the hunt for my glasses and joined her on the couch.

'Turns out,' she continued, 'that we were both pregnant at the same time but she and John decided not to tell us in case it added to my stress levels, and then after our miscarriage, because they thought it might somehow deepen our grief. She has reached the stage when her bump is starting to show, and she felt that she had to, and in better circumstances would have loved to, tell me.'

The silence was not tactical this time. I didn't know what to say. I was searching for the right question. If there was one. I was thinking of how to spin Molly's news in a way that would help and at the same time protect Dannielle and allow her to get some purchase on her best friend's pregnancy. If there was a way. I was waiting for the best time to pick up the conversation. There wasn't one.

'I feel terrible now,' said Danny. 'I should have climbed over the table, knocking cakes to the floor, and thrown my arms around her so that we could jump up and down like footballers who win a corner do. But I froze when I should have been full of warmth towards Molly. What must she think? I have been so selfish and bloody self-pitying.'

'Don't be hard on yourself, darling. Molly knew that the news would have an impact, she expected it to. That's why she has put off telling you until she no longer could. Can you imagine how hard it has been for Molly to keep this from you, and probably everyone else, in case we found out from someone other than themselves?'

'You're right,' said Dannielle, lifting her head and throwing her shoulders back. 'Can we go around to hers now, hun? I want to do the football thing.'

'Do you want to, or do you just think you should do?' I asked.

'I really want to. Let's pick up a couple of those hideous it's a girl balloons on the way. Molly loves them. She also loves any type of free wine, so let's pick some of that up as well, after paying for it.'

'You're amazing, darling. And if you are looking for another positive, you have survived nearly thirty miles in the passenger seat of a vehicle driven by Molly Knievel!'

'I'm surprised she could drive at all,' said Dannielle, 'with a pullover on that must have been discarded by Giant Haystacks.

'On the perilous car journey back,' Dannielle revealed, 'Molly was doing a U-turn when she told me she has a terrible sense of direction, and *she didn't know where that came from*, because her dad was a lorry driver. Funny and typical Molly. We had to pull into a lay-by when I explained to her just how funny that was.'

Hidden from Dannielle, I summoned a tone reserved for happy hearing. 'Hi, Mollers, just checking you're both in. Fantastic news about the baby, we're absolutely made up for you.'

'Thank you, thank you, thank you, Stephen.'

'Erm, listen, Moll, Dannielle feels really bad about the way she took your news earlier and wants to visit you.'

'Of course. Amazing, in fact. She has no need to feel bad, tell her. John's here, would you like to speak with him?'

'Absolutely, but not immediately,' I answered.

A no-doubt-puzzled Molly asked, 'When would you like to come over?'

'Now, see you in thirty. One last thing, promise me you will be at least six feet from anything expensive when she arrives.' Click. Followed by more puzzlement.

'John, put some trousers on, please, baby, for once. The Cunninghams are on the way. Stephen was talking in riddles on the phone for some reason.'

'Moll, what rhymes with maybe, and will also visit soon?'

'Don't you start, I'm already confused. I don't know, tell me.'

'No wonder you couldn't understand Stephen. You are a riddle all of your own, my darling. But I love you for some reason,' said John.

'Thank you, baby. Come on, what is the answer?'

*

'Come in, come in,' said John.

'Nice trousers, mate. Everything comes back into fashion if you are prepared to wait long enough,' I said, sartorially aloof.

The second riddle about the requirement for sufficient space was solved as soon as Danny met Molly. I shook John's hand as the girls (jumping up and down and rotating simultaneously like footballers do) celebrated a goal that will put Molly 2-1 up, with still lots of time to play.

'Leave your shirts on, girls. You don't want a yellow card,' said Mr Fashion.

'My goodness, Versace, you've changed,' I said.

Molly rang her friend and neighbour and asked if she could throw Sam and Martin into her car when she collected her own seven-year-old problem from school, leaving us clear to show our best friends that we were their best friends over wine and nibbles and beneath two ridiculously large-but- reasonably-priced barrage balloons.

When Martin and Sam arrived home, our topic of conversation led to Sam saying, 'We got showed aaallll about how babies happen in school today.'

Hands straight to their mouths; uncontrollable, unnecessarily loud laughter before upstairs to the TV.

'I don't remember anything about babies at school today, Sam.'

'Me neither. But thanks for laughing downstairs like you did. I heard some of the older girls talking about baby making yesterday, and they were laughing and doing what we do with our hands, so there must be something funny about it.'

Chapter 47

At home, Dannielle told me that rather than being something to be jealous about, Molly's news was positive and perhaps even encouraging.

'Don't tell Molly I told you, promise, please don't, but due to an allegedly never-before- experienced functional blip in his baby making department, well, a six-month blip in the whole store, actually, they sought advice from a baby clinic who were able to help John regain some semblance of respect in the bedroom. If you call him Limp Dick next time we see them, I'll kill you.

'In addition, tests had revealed that John's sperm count was low-ish and that despite having his stiffy back, which was good news in itself, for both of them, there was no guarantee that his payload would reach the factory, so to speak.

'So imagine their happiness,' she continued, 'when after many attempted parcel deliveries, she tested positive. She reckons that the decision to try for a baby was taken at least eighteen months before conception. Are you with me?'

'Indeed,' I slobbered. 'And if you would consider slipping your work clothes on, I could be with you right now, baby! Sorry, a bit loud that.'

Later, as Dannielle's physio costume lay strewn and in some places torn across our bedroom floor, in the downstairs hallway, all the way up the stairs and on the landing (she wore more clothes at work than I had thought), and she lay asleep, thoroughly, utterly exhausted but content, I thought how useful the word lay is when describing these circumstances, how many weeks there were in a blip and at what age a baby clinic becomes an adult clinic.

Chapter 48

I placed the almost identical kangaroo letters in date order and numbered them 1–8 for easy reference. Kangaroos do have a knack of looking similar, don't they. An identification parade would be of little evidential value in the Woolloomooloo Animal Sanctuary, in the northern south/east region of Western Australia and home to over 500 very similar kangaroos. To make things even less appetising to prosecutors, the flyers (or mums) of the species named the Eastern grey kangaroo almost always give birth to twins and occasionally triplets that are therefore related, grey and incredibly similar to one another.

I digress slightly. Call *Letter One*.

> Gooday Dad, how ya goin? I hope you're well. It's one hundred degrees Fahrenheit out here. My mate Zac has gone walkabout and I'm lookin after his crib while he's away. I miss you, mate, and thought it might be nice if we could keep in touch, particularly now as you're getting older. Zac's address is on the back of the envelope. I'm going to be here for at least six months, probably longa.
>
> Can't remember ever writing a letter before so I feel a bit rusty. I've cracked open a tinny in the hope that the lager will help me. It's a no-brainer, because even if it doesn't help me I'm still drinkin it.

'Hi, hun, anything interesting so far?'

'No, darling, it's more like the back of a postcard than a letter, but early days.'

'Coffee?'

'Yes, please, Sheila. Unless you have any chilled Fosters. No worries if you don't.'

I'm enjoyin it enough out here, Dad, but one of Mum's Sunday lunches wouldn't go amiss. Instead the Indian Ocean and miles and miles of sun soaked sandy beaches are a close second best. Well, I've run out of words and lager, Dad, but at least I've got this letter thing started. I hope you find time to write back. That would be ripper.

Love Phillip

'Flippin', or should it be, Phillipin' 'eck, Danners, it's like listening to Jason Donovan. That's not exactly lengthy for an introductory, is it?'
    Don't forget you're picking Loud Mouth up in thirty minutes,' she said quietly.
    No worries, Sheila, I'll just read one more, exhibit *L2*, in fact, then I'll go on driveabout. Do you need anything whilst I'm out?'
    No thank you, you Crocodile, you ripper, but you may like to get some 4X for the barbie.'

Gooday, Dad, how you goin?
    Thanks for your letter, I don't think I've ever seen your handwriting before. Did you use a fountain pen? Nice. Sorry to hear you're not enjoying retirement. That's normal I would think when you have been someone and now you're not, so to speak. That sort of came out different to what I meant, sorry. I wasn't surprised to hear that you and Mum weren't getting along too well now you are in each other's pockets, as you put it. It's a big adjustment from the routine of work life. It might be difficult for her too, don't forget.
    I've got a chance of a job coming up and if I get it I'm out of Zac's and into my own place. Zac is not exactly Mr straight and narrow if you get my Rorkes, and I'm going to get caught up in it if I stay here when he comes back. I hate being in someone else's crib, I can't wait to have my own, so keep your fingers crossed for

me. Temperatures are still in the high nineties, and I hear the beach and a barbie calling. I will write again soon. Keep your kookaburras chirping.

Luvya. Phillip

'I'm off, darling. I'll run by the creek on the way home and grab a bottle of Australian Yellow Tail Shiraz. Back soon. No need to look for the bottle opener, Sheila, I'll rip the cork out with my teeth. That's where the term Ripper comes from, you know, you little beaut.'

Anything in *L2*?' she asked.

No, I don't think I can be bothered with the others. I feel like I'm prying, to be perfectly honest, like a mother reading her daughter's diary, or like searching Snowy's bed for my neck support.'

Fair dinkum,' she said. 'I'm fed up with the Australian references anyway.'

*

Mum rang me on the car phone. 'Hello, dear. Anything in the letters?'

No, Mum, distant son-to-dad things only. Why the interest?'

I haven't seen Phillip for so long. I'm interested to find out what he's up to down there.'

Unknown so far, to me at stage *L2*, she couldn't have put it better.

Hello, Muffs, climb in. How you goin'?' I asked in a more South African than Australian accent.

What does that mean?' he asked.

It means how are you? How has your day been?' I asked.

Why do you ask?' he asked.

That is what dads ask sons outside school,' I explained.

I ask you. What is the point of any attempt at conversation with a nearly-eight-year-old?

Glad you brought my ear muffs, Daddy. How you goin'?'

He looked like a Doctor Who Cyberman with those white ear muffs on. Later that night, I was to search my Tardis for the book, *Fifty Ways to Incapacitate a Cyberman, Without Hurting Him Too Much.*

Chapter 49

L3.

Hi Dad, how are you? [Is he back in Blighty? I thought.]

Hope you're well. Thanks for your letta. No betta with Mum then. [He's still there.] Lots of older people forget things so don't worry about that. Can I mention that Zac's dad passed away last year without leaving a will. Don't leave yourself in that position, Dad, before your memory gets any worse. Probate is difficult, lengthy and expensive, and his mum, who was here yesterday, is going through hell with their two warring daughters over it all.

Listen, I didn't get that job. Zac is back earlier than expected and the only money I get is by making some deliveries for his business. I've got another mate who has offered to put me up but on a couch, not in a bedroom. No good with my back. To add to it, a lady I have been seeing for only two months has announced that she is pregnant and that she wants to keep the baby. Wish I'd stayed home sometimes to be honest. Anyway, look after yourself, Pops. I'll be fine. I'm sure this difficult period will pass for both of us.

Love ya, Dad. Phillip X

'Darling, would you read this, please? It starts in English, not Australian like the first two, for some reason.'

'You look serious. What's the matter, hun?'

'It's only short,' I said, 'like Phillip. Please read it and tell me what you think. I know what I think.'

'Well, he's got problems out there, hasn't he. When was this letter written?' she asked.

'2020, early 2020, about five or six years after Dad's retirement,' I said.

I rang Mum. 'Mum, I'm reading through your favourite son's letters. Dad did leave a will, didn't he?'

'I've told you he did. That's why I tried to contact Phillip.'

'You contacted Phillip to tell him his dad was dead. You told me *he* raised the issue of the will.'

'You're shouting at me for some reason, Stephen, questioning me, cross-examining me. Stop it. I don't like it.'

She put the phone down.

It was late. Mum was right; I was shouting rather than asking. I told Dannielle I would call on Mum on the way home from work the next day to apologise. Dannielle was cross, concerned and forthright.

'Don't leave it that long, Stephen. Either ring her back right now, which I would do, or ring her before work tomorrow. I don't blame her if she doesn't answer. I wouldn't.'

I rang her back. She answered.

'I'm sorry, Mum, really sorry. I love you. See you at about four thirty tomorrow when I'll explain. I'm probably jumping to conclusions,' I said.

But I wasn't.

'Bedtime, Poirot. Work tomorrow, for both of us,' said Dannielle. 'Maybe you are jumping to conclusions, hun,' she said. 'The next letter may vindicate you [it does], but don't blame your mum, it's unfair. Just because she is the only one of the trilogy that you can talk to, or have a go at, don't treat her like a punchbag, like you just have.'

*

I awoke at 4 am. I couldn't sleep and I opened *L4*.

> Dad, I'm in the shit. Please help. I lost one of Zac's packages and didn't make an important business delivery. The intended recipient is big time in a bad way. He has given me two weeks to pay him 5,000 dollars or suffer the consequences. I know that you've more than looked after me in your will but please, can you help me with this? I have no other way of finding that sort of

money without raiding a bank. I'm scared, Dad, my life is in danger. Please help.

One last thing, Dad, make sure you have your will checked over by a solicitor in case you-know-who contests it.

Love you. Phillip X

PS I have enclosed my bank account details below for your convenience. Make sure that your will starts with being of sound mind.

PPS Zac's mum has signed her home into Zac's ownership to protect her from massive care home fees. Might be worth looking into.

*

At breakfast. 'How much is a return flight to Australia, darling? Do you know?'

'Why do you ask, hun?'

'Because my devious, much smaller brother needs a damn good beating, from me. You might like to read that,' I said, slamming *L4* on a worktop.

'Well, to me that's just a continuation of his bad luck, and maybe asking the Bank of Mum and Dad to help out is understandable in the circumstances.'

'Darling, sometimes...'

I emailed Beth to tell her that I was working from home, and available if required.

L5.

Hi Dad. Thanks for the money. So grateful. It has meant that I have paid for the lost package, got out of trouble for now at least and got my own flat. No more deliveries for me, I hope. I'm glad to hear in your letter that the will is airtight. That must be such a relief for you. Did you check out the ins and outs of signing Mum's house over to me to protect her if she is widowed?

My new address is on the back of the envelope. You should see this place, Dad. It's amazing. Better than

Zac's. The rent is going to find a bit of raising further down the line but thanks to you, the first six months are paid for, with enough left over to feed and clothe me, until I find a job.

I promise I will find a way of paying you back, Dad. Love you. Anyway, can't stop, it's beach time again, Dad, ninety degrees Fahrenheit, the best burgers in the world and ladies that don't overdress. Paradise. Speak to you soon.

PS Your spelling isn't what it used to be and you spelt my name wrong. Ha ha. XX

L6.

Thanks for your letter, Dad. It was a little confusing but I got the gist of it. You mustn't worry about what Stephen thinks. He has hardly ever visited, has he? I bet you haven't seen your grandson, Michael, is it, since he was a baby. Stephen only lives five miles from your house and passes yours on the way home from work. He and Dannielle are both working and are not short of a few bob, let's put it that way. I had the bollocks to travel halfway around the world in search of a job. Don't forget that. Zac once asked me, in a rare moment of interest, if I would return home for your funeral. I hope it's a long way off, Dad, but I promise you nothing will keep me away. Write to you soon. Love you. Your favourite son.

Phillip XX

L7.

Thanks for your letter, Dad. You need a spell check in your head. I thought I was bad. Ha ha. I've noticed that more money has gone into my bank account. Thank you. Every little helps as they say. No luck on the job front. Bad news on the flat front, Dad. The management company have informed me of a massive increase in charges that are beyond me. I have never been happier to live somewhere than where I am now, Dad. I can't bear the thought of leaving my home. Not after all I have been through.

I hear what you say about the short messages from my end, but that's the way I hang. If I was an author, I would favour short stories over novels.

Love you, Dad. Thanks again.

Phillip XX

L8.

Wow. Thanks for the money and for sight of your will, Dad. I see that you have confirmed that you were of sound mind when you signed it and that it was signed in front of witnesses. Good on ya. What a comfort for you. I had no idea that you had amounted such a sum. Respect mate. I can't thank you enough.

Stop worrying about Stephen, he has more than enough money of his own. Your decision to exclude him from an inheritance and put money in a trust for his son was your decision, the right decision in my view. I'm surprised you even recognise Stephen these days. Try not to worry about losing things or about your blood pressure. You might consider taking your car off the road though. If your writing is anything to go by, you could be a danger to other drivers. Lol.

Leaving the house to Mum, with the caveat, is a no-brainer. I hope she spends many more years in your home, if she outlives you. How is she by the way? I'm not good at letters, Dad. That's why I don't waffle on. I like to keep things short and sweet.

Phillip XXX

These are demands, I thought, not letters. Pre-meditated, incrementally emotional blackmail. Loosely camouflaged and clearly intended to entrap a man susceptible to persuasion and coercion. He is stealing from his own Father, Mother and Brother right there.

At the offices of Phillips, Redmond and Burns Solicitors, Mr Rodney Redmond, Esq. KC LLB himself, declared that all those before him (me and Mum) should take recognisance and recognise that the estate of my late father, properly exchanged and witnessed, had been, with the exception of the matrimonial dwelling, subject to the late addendum at 12(2) below, and a small trust to be referred to later is left 'in totum' to his son, Phillip Wilson Cunningham, Resident of Western Australia.

The late addendum referred to, specified circumstances whereby any true diagnosis of mental decline in any form or measure of my mother, or upon her death, will result in the transference of the ownership of the marital home to the aforementioned Phillip Wilson Cunningham.

How can that be allowed? I thought. The legal terms attached in humour only days earlier by the wife of Phillip's late victim will be sharpened up, and attached, I assure you, 'ut gravitas' to a contentious probate claim in which the will will be both challenged and contested. There is a difference.

As well as providing Mum and me with our day in court, the minimum of twelve months' associated legal argument and decision ahead, which may drag on beyond that, will prevent Phillip, at least in the short-to-medium term, from using the proceeds of his crime to extricate himself from the probably criminal hole that he has got himself into. I'm sure the wonderful charitable Zac will lend him a shovel. I would love to be there when he receives the letter from Mr Redmond KC informing him of our action. I would love to be allowed to insert a note saying, *Daddy can't finance you out of this one, Smartarse.*

I ask you, what sort of man manipulates his fading father from the other side of the world, and swindles his mother and brother out of almost half a million pounds in inheritance? A selfish, criminal one; that's what sort of man my brother is. In the event that Mum and I have the opportunity to face him in court, it would be in his own interests to be behind a screen. Civil courts steer clear of such protection for respondents but, believe me, he will know that I am there, in his eyeline. If Mum is still alive, the prospect of giving evidence and seeing her sons in public confrontation will place an enormous strain on her. Another effect of her favourite son's actions.

With encouragement from me, our solicitor was at great pains to explain the emotional, intellectual and financial burden the challenge will bring.

'Mum,' I said, 'we can proceed without you. You don't have to put yourself through this, you *may* think [I chose against using the phrase you *must* think] he has caused you enough upset. I will handle the costs and we will get them back when we win.' (I hoped.)

*

'I have been listening carefully to you, Mr Thornberry Esq. LLB,' she replied confidently. 'I have given this a great deal of thought. Phillip Wilson Cunningham, or the respondent as I now prefer to call him, has [glancing at me] embezzled our future. When his father was truly of sound mind, before he was deceived, he had often spoken to me, and to his late brother, about the proceeds of his will and how he took great satisfaction from declaring that a busy, well-paid life had left him in the very fortunate position to be able to distribute many thousands of pounds amongst me, Stephen and the respondent, and to ensure that I would always have a roof over my head, without a late addendum.

'By the time some of those letters arrived, probably before then, Mr Thornberry, he was putting postage stamps on the back of envelopes, if you follow my drift. Of the fifty marbles he had before all of this, he lost one, sometimes two, every month. Including some of his most favourite. You don't have to be Ironside to understand the value of my intimate and accurate assessment of his state of mind, given on oath by what I will portray as a timid, vulnerable, cheated but mentally sound old woman.

'Mr Thornberry, I hope that means I have passed the potential witness assessment that you have been engaged in, rather indelicately at times. You must be surprised I have remembered your name. You have no need to talk more slowly to me than to Stephen, or with a raised voice, if you don't mind. I pray that I will still have full cognisance for the next two years.'

A second glance at me allowed her sight of my very best so-proud-of-you look.

A significant glance, more of a glare actually, at our host drew a sincere response from Mr T.

'Forgive me, Mrs Cunningham, I meant no offence and I will always act in your best interests [as long as you pay me]. I will apply my mind to this case and I will instruct a specialist barrister to lead. Thank you, both.

'I will keep you updated between now and our next meeting. Proof of service of a writ on the respondent is crucial. I will inform you when that has occurred. Good day to you.'

Chapter 50

'Do you think my mum and your mum might enjoy us treating them to a pub lunch, darling?' I asked.

'My mum really appreciates gestures like that, hun,' said Danners, 'and despite warning me post-puberty that there is no such thing as a free lunch where men are concerned, she will jump at the opportunity.'

'Bit like when we first met then, eh, eh … baby?' I said.

'Seriously though, darling, my mum is dying for an update on the Kangaroo Papers as she calls them, and if the music is right and the weather fair, Grandma Flatley might take the chance to fly again and to land on grass rather than on her couch.'

'Can't me and Snowy come?' asked Martin, using a suitable expression learnt from Snowy.

'Of course, mate, you and the snow man are always invited, although you will have to pay for your own lunch,' I said, using a suitable expression learnt from Dannielle. Turns out that what I thought was a suitable expression was either poorly thrown or was misread, and drew the comment, 'You're a mean daddy.'

'Where do you fancy, darling?' I asked.

'Somewhere in the country, with a canal and tethered boats with names like *Willow Tree* or *Freedom* and a mountain much bigger than that Penny something one near Ingleton. One point nine miles east of Horton in Ribblesdale,' my spatially aware darling answered.

'I'm not going,' said Martin, defiantly.

'You'll be here on your own,' I said in a spooky voice.

'Snowy will stay with me,' he countered.

'Oh no, he won't. Not if I say w a l k i e s and d u c k s out loud.'

'I'll stay on my own then.'

'What if I say i c e-a-c r e a m-a?'

'Snowy won't understand that, hun,' spluttered my mid-croissant, very-pleased-with-herself wife.

'I was only joking, Muffs. Your mum will pay for you and anything Snowy fancies devouring, won't you, darling?'

Rather than spell her reply in case Martin heard it, she flicked a commonly used hand sign from a pocket and asked me if they were mine.

By then, Martin was in the garden with Snow Man. He was getting no response when spelling the word d u c k s. The trick, you see, is to say the word walkies first.

After receiving confirmations from Messrs Cunningham and Flatley, I booked the canalside, duck-infested, ice cream-packed Shady Oak country pub. No mountain, but two castles on adjacent hills. Then, as a group, we looked forward to it.

*

The following day, I asked my mate Graham in graphics to knock up a nameplate with the word *Freedom* emblazoned upon it, in that nearly endearing, boating-at-4-knots, grapevine-infested, pastel-coloured style popular with canal people, complete with heavy duty Blu Tack, known as glue tack, obviously. I also had something else in mind.

Chapter 51

On a warmish, dry Saturday morning, 06.00hrs, at Tate Hill, a sheltered sandy beach, nestled beside the River Esk and 1.4 miles from Whitby, where dogs are allowed all year round. A wonderful spot for sandcastle building, seaweed sifting, dune dancing and head clearing. Snow Man and I went ahead because he was going nuts after I whispered the word walkies to him before shouting the word ducks.

'Why didn't Snowy go mad when I said ducks, Mummy?'

'Because your dad is silly, son. I've figured out how he does it. I'll show you later,' was the firstly accurate then spoily sporty reply.

Quick territory marker on a tree, brief sniff of a post and down the far-from-gradual stairway to the beach. Then at top speed, ears back, nose wet, tongue out, straight into the water. Snowy stayed on the beach.

This was a place of memories. Dannielle and I had enjoyed many a romantic moonlit stroll, pausing to kiss whilst hand in hand, with other people before we met at a barn dance. I had gone into the water wearing shorts on this morning, which was more than I was wearing on one of the aforementioned strolls without Dannielle. On a night when the water wasn't too cold, obviously.

Jet, a more appropriately named black Labrador, was ignoring his owner's commands to return to her in favour of Snowy's company. The usual stiff stance, nose-to-nose, I'm-in-charge-here-mate, my-tail-is-more-erect-than-yours, don't-call-me-mate posturing soon gave way to a deliberate joint attempt at the world record make-themselves-as-dirty-and-as-smelly-as possible title. Snowy was really good at it, really good. Jet's owner joined me. Now, I gave up looking at other women in that way many moons ago on instruction from Danny, but if I hadn't been the subject of such constraint, I would most definitely have looked at this woman. We walked on as a foursome for a few minutes whilst the rest of my family caught up. My new walking friend looked at her bleeping watch and said, 'Please excuse me. Must go. We are here every weekday at this time, nice to meet you.'

I dropped my pace to allow my followers to reach me.

Well, didn't I get it in the beachcombers!

'Who's that?'

'I've no idea, darling,' I replied, honestly.

'I wondered why you flew down those steps quicker than Snowy. Spoilt your fun, have I?'

'What do you mean?'

'The steps down to the beach.'

'No, the second part about spoiling my fun.'

'Just a coincidence, is it, that Snowy, who has *never* played with another dog in his whole bloody life, happens to take an interest in the dog that was passing by with her?' (Pointing towards a disappearing her.)

'Well, there is a dog called Missie that he happily plays with, but putting that aside, what on earth are you getting at?' I asked, knowing the answer.

'Mrs Wetsuit, fancy pants, Pamela Anderson tribute act over there.' (More pointing over there but this time with a flicking movement.)

'Oh. I see now,' I said. 'Pammy has just received a call-out to a swimmer in distress in Whitby. She has to slip out of that tight wetsuit and into a red well-fitting swimsuit first before heading up there. Otherwise, I'm sure she would have confirmed, if asked, that it was Jet's misbehaviour that brought us together.'

'Jet? So you admit that there was misbehaviour and you just happened to know her dog's name after ten seconds. Was it just a lucky guess? No wonder Snowy was excited. He knew that Jet was out here waiting to get thoroughly covered in sand with him, didn't he.'

The swimmer, more accurately the poor swimmer, had made it ashore at Whitby. Jet's owner and Jet were no longer walking away from us. Snowy and Jet resumed Operation Filth. Jet's owner, whose name I was about to discover was also Dannielle, and her dog approached.

'Oh my God,' my Dannielle cried before embracing fancy pants Pamela Anderson as if she had just scored at Wembley.

I was in the clear. It transpired that my wife, who had only recently told me that she trusted me more than life itself, was dancing with a former acquaintance who had come on to her, almost successfully, apparently, and hopefully, sorry, at university. Forgive me, some inappropriate thoughts passed through my mind right there that only another heterosexual man would understand. And some perverts perhaps.

A filthy smelly companion, Snowy and Jet were abandoned whilst the ladies screwed themselves into the soft sand.

'How have you got in that state, Muffs?' I asked.

'Mum was dragging me along the beach,' he answered. 'I couldn't get to my feet when you were talking to the lady she is dancing with. I need to check another word with you later, Dad.'

'Learn from that, Muffs. Women are very difficult to understand, impossible, actually. Don't ever waste your time trying. Just know when to pretend to give in. That's the secret. Any time you need advice, I'm here for you. I have a master's degree in Dannielle Cunningham.'

Our Dannielle and her friend Dannielle, and you must forgive me for more of those inappropriate thoughts if you are not a red-blooded male, continued celebrating their reunion. After I prized them apart, shouting break, I explained to Martin that in certain circumstances, and this was one of them, and always in front of me, it was okay for two athletic women to hug and kiss each other. First standing and circling, and then prone, lying on the sand, even for that long, on a Saturday morning.

Dannielle, the woman who had innocently threatened to smash my marriage to my Dannielle to pieces, was invited, with her wife, to join us for dinner.

A thought lingered. Why did she tell me that she was on the beach every weekday morning – before she hugged Danny? She explained later that Jet had never before played with another dog. That was why.

'Goodness me, Danners, you were quick to jump to conclusions there. I refuse to go on a walk along a beach near Whitby, on a warmish Saturday morning, one hundred yards ahead of you, with the snow man, ever again.'

'I'm sorry, hun. Shall I put my physio outfit on later by way of apology?' she asked.

Gotcha, she thought.

Typical woman's trick, that. Using my lust to her advantage. She now had a tailor-made, post- flare up let's-be-friends strategy that I would just have to learn to live with. There is no such thing as a free walk on a beach where Dannielle is concerned. Flatley didn't tell her that, did she?

Chapter 52

Mobile to mobile.

'I have a cunning plan, mate, as Baldrick used to say.'

'Fire away,' said John.

'You mentioned that your dad's birthday is coming up later this month.'

'Yep. A week on Sunday. He'll be seventy-two, why?'

'It's time to reveal my cunning plan.'

'Can't wait. I've fallen victim to your Baldrick thinking in the past, so you're frightening me. What is it?'

'Well, no need to be frightened here, Robocop. You were thinking of using the occasion of his birthday to prize him out of his flat, weren't you? By coincidence, honestly, Danny and I are treating our mums to lunch at your favourite, tranquil, quant, nicely painted canalside pub where the food is reasonably priced, a week on Sunday, and it might do him the world of good if all three last of the summer winers were to join us.

'Having two other decrepit, slightly deaf old timers, one with broken reading glasses, might be good for him. My mum's still reeling from the letters, Danny's mum is only just beginning to come to terms with the curtains coming down on her show before they went up, and your dad, erm, well, it won't do him any harm to get some fresh air. What do you think, Blackadder?'

'My first thought is that your plan has too many words in it,' said John. 'My second thought is that it might just work. What does Dannielle think?'

'It is a secret cunning plan, Rowbow. She doesn't know about it, and if Molly finds out, we might as well put it on the front page of the *Yorkshire Chronicle*.'

'So, help me with this, Balders,' said John. 'You expect Cagney and Lacey to accept this as a coincidence. That we have made similar plans to you, for the same day, at a pub fifteen miles away from your home, that you have never visited before?'

'Not for one second, John, so we must both prepare to employ the fingers-across-the-throat, say-nothing hand signal at our first opportunity after the coincidence is detected, so that the winers remain oblivious. I'll take Cagney, and I'll cover you as you take your Lacey.'

'Do you know, mate,' said John again, 'it might just work if I can tempt Tommy the troglodyte from his cave, which won't be easy. I visited him yesterday and he is still low. He told me he would like some company now and then but can't handle being in company for any length of time anymore.'

'Well, I have a good feeling about this, John. Even if it goes wrong, I get to eat crispy edged roasties; lamb; thick, almost treacly, viscous gravy and mint sauce.'

'If it goes wrong, Stevo, you will be wearing roasties; lamb; treacly, viscous gravy and mint sauce. Nevertheless, let's do it. I'll ring the landlord, Gordon, who we have got to know quite well, and book it for half one. I'll ask him to put screens around our tables as a precaution.'

'Good news is, Baldrick,' John said, 'that they do have viscous gravy on the menu.'

Chapter 53

Phone call, landline to mobile.

'Stephen, I've found another letter, or rather the lady in the charity shop has found another letter, in the pocket of one of the coats I donated, if that's the right word. She was kind enough to deliver it to me by hand this morning.'

'Have you read it, Mum?'

'I can't even bear to touch it, son.'

'I understand, I'll call in on my way home. Don't be fretting, Mum. It can't be any worse than the others, and it might help our case in the same way they have.'

It did.

L9.

> *Hi Dad. I hope you enjoy the Algarve. I'll wait until you get back before writing again. Were you a bit tipsy when you wrote your last letter? Your handwriting started off in capitals and changed halfway through to a much smaller lower case? Do you own that apartment, out of interest?*
>
> *I can't thank you enough for the standing order, Daddio. Having that regular funding will be so cool. It means I can stay in my crib, buy some snazzy furniture and help support the baby when it arrives. If it's a boy, we are going to name it after you. He'll be the only boy in his school called Dad!*
>
> *I'll be able to save some of it. You're a ripper. A thought has occurred to me, Dad. It occurred to Zac actually. It wouldn't have occurred to me. I don't like the*

thought of anyone else reading our letters at some time in the future. We are very private people, aren't we, you even more than me, and what we have shared is between you and me. Nobody else's business. Father to son only. Very, VERY private. I'm sure you agree. I repeat, nobody else's business. You will be better off destroying them. I'm sure you agree, don't you? I hope I have made myself clear.

Luvya. Phillip XXX

I had read the letter out loud.

'Could be worse, couldn't it, Mum?'

'Is worse,' said Mum, tearfully.

Minutes later, two lovely cups of tea, one with sugar, were trying to make things better for us.

Mum was staring at the open letter next to the tea on the coffee table. 'I am lost for words to describe *that*,' she said.

'I know that our solicitor will consider it gold dust, and now I am committed to the case, so do I. But that doesn't make it any the less painful to hear your husband being brainwashed by his son.'

Chapter 54

The Friday before my cunning plan was to be tested.

Mr Thornberry rang. 'Our agent in Australia is having difficulty serving papers on the respondent. He called at the address supplied and was greeted by a gentleman who purported to be one Zac Goldsmith. Of course, I assume this to be the Zac referred to in the letters exhibited as *L1* to *L9* incl.

'The agent has described said gentleman as white, small, slim, maybe only five foot six, with thinning hair and a pronounced red birthmark on his neck, below his left ear.'

'Please inform said agent,' I said, 'that he has met Phillip Cunningham, and to serve said papers on him should he ever see him again. Which is now unlikely.

'I could have supplied a ten-year-old photograph if asked that clearly exhibits the birthmark on his neck. Basic stuff for a bounty hunter, I would have thought. I'm disappointed and annoyed in equal measure, Mr Thornberry.'

With that news, the outcome of this particular thread was consigned to my next book, along with the contents of the diary and the notebook. One entry in the notebook will be of great significance.

*

John's dad's birthday. The weather was promising enough for me to entertain the thought that our screened-off tables might be outside. Blissfully unaware, Cagney and Lacey were slobbing around in their onesies.

John rang. 'Dad's playing up, mate, but I think he's going to come. Either way, Molly, Sam and me will see you there behind the screens, which, initially at least, will make it difficult to see you there.'

Everything was going well at my end of the deceit. My mum had promised not to ask Flatley to perform her teapot thing, or perform full stop, actually. She was also asked not to mention that she had joined a marvellous spinsters' club, which she wished she had joined before her husband passed away.

Martin and Sam were warned to keep their language in check and the snow man was told that duck hunting was unlawful outside the duck hunting season, and that we were outside it.

'How is your dad playing, Danners?' I asked.

'Well, Mum has given him a little latitude early doors. No yellows yet.'

'Refs do that to keep a game flowing, darling.'

'How interesting. Broadly speaking, she is happy with the way things are going. Nothing is perfect, *is it,* dear?' (Cue raised eyebrows look.)

'Should we have invited him to the Shady Oak, do you think?'

'Just as well we didn't,' she answered. 'Mum is still mildly ashamed of being seen in public with him and she told me earlier that he came home from a crucial dominoes game last night, which they lost, unfit to be anywhere near a canal, any cutlery, a child or a dog for many days to come.

'A yellow card with a red border, left by Mona, on the last stair before the hallway, rather than flashed at him in the usual manner, silently awaited his receipt, and I quote:

'When or if you climb out of your hole, in her absence.'

'That's good, not for him, of course. We'll leave at twelve forty-five, gang. Please be ready.'

I was having second thoughts, a sort of pre-match tension if you like. I was imagining the range of reactions available to Dannielle, from appreciative laughter all the way through to murder. The satnav was set, and I said to my travelling executioner (excuse the well-founded pessimism), 'Well, let's see if one of Bonnie and Clyde's recommendations finally matches your cooking standards, Nigella, and scores well on your nice-place tick sheet.'

A risky one, that, to someone who struggles with cheese and pickle sandwiches, but by mentioning them, I hoped that it was helping, in a small perhaps subliminal way, to prepare Pierrepoint for the prospect of being stood down, at least for today.

*

'Are we nearly there yet?' asked Mona.

'He never tells the truth when you ask him that one, Nanna,' said the child who holds the world record for asking that question on one journey.

'Our bladder control isn't as good as we would like these days, is it, dear?' Mona added, looking for support from my hitherto continent mum.

A glance from Pierrepoint shared what she was thinking, which was, let's hope the control of what she says at the Oak is more controlled than her control of her bladder. (Molly had taught us both *mindreading for beginners.*)

On arrival, a nearly full car park made my nerves jangle still further at the prospect of a free-to- view, very-well-attended bun fight with menaces.

Deliberately, I had arrived early to approach one of the barge people and ask them to tack the nameplate to their vessel. [I hadn't told John about this part of the plan] So, I sat my passengers at one of the screened-off tables before returning to the car to collect said item and a bottle of red by way of reward.

Three of the four boats moored along the bank were in an area obscured from the screen dwellers' view. My luck was in, and so were boat owners Shaun and partner Nicky. They were leisurely preparing for take-off at around 1.45 pm, and the roar of the boat's twin-stroke underpowered engine attracted no one's attention. Lovely couple, who had said hello to me before I said hello to them. After easily coercing them, Shaun explained that this sort of childishness was right up his street.

The nameplate was attached and Shaun leant a brush against it to complete the temporary high-tech attachment to his boat, which was now temporarily named *Freedom.*

'Shaun,' I said, 'may I take further advantage of your childish nature?'

'Of course, but it will have to be quick. We are off to pastures new very shortly.' I explained his role before returning to the screen people.

Right on cue, Shaun appeared and exclaimed, 'Stevo, how are you, mate? You know Nicky, don't you.'

'Of course I do. You haven't changed one bit, Nicky,' I said, seeing her for the second time in my life.

'How are my favourite seafarers then? What were the chances of seeing you two here?'

'Next to nil, mate, a million to one, more chance of hell freezing over.' (Don't overdo it, Nelson. Stick to the script.)

'We should have left at seven this morning.' (Award winning, Shaun, my mate, very convincing role play. There was a place for this talent with the Padgate Players.)

I introduced my party in the genre of Les – *I really don't know* – Dennis on *Family Fortunes*, before Shaun apologised for his swift departure to *Freedom*.

'Lovely to meet you all,' he said. 'Wish we could stay longer, Stevo,' before bidding us goodbye.

'I've still got your number somewhere, mate. I'll give you a ring,' I said in the warmest of tones. My annoying habit of adding an ers to a person's name, such as Moll<u>ers</u> and Dann<u>ers,</u> was inappropriate on this occasion so, 'Lovely to meet you again, Nick,' was my tack. An appropriate word in the circumstances. Better if *Freedom* had been a yacht.

'Weren't they lovely,' said my mum.

'Absolutely lovely, nice to have a surprise like that,' said Mona. 'Where do you know them from, Stevo?' (wry smile)

'Shaun used to be an IT wizard in our offices. He left earlier this year after an inheritance allowed him to live the dream on his mini cruise liner.' Oops, my first slip. Mum didn't like the word inheritance anymore.

Completely taken in, my Cagney puzzled, 'I'm sure I've met him before, hun. He seemed familiar.'

'Well, that's the real reason why he had to leave, actually, but he has been at the last three Christmas parties, two of them without

Nickers. You might have met him, or may have been pestered by him then.'

'Yep. Thought so, I remember him now. He hasn't changed a bit either, and I didn't feel pestered.' (wry wink)

'Can I see their boat, Daddy?'

'Of course, son. They'll be passing here shortly and we can give them a wave.' Another clever use of a nautical term on my part.

'You'll have to be ready, son. These speedsters don't dwell on a swell.'

Another one. It's a gift.

'Oh, you're not going to believe this, guys,' exclaimed Dannielle. 'It never rains coincidences but it pours. Look who's here. That's Molly's car being driven by John.'

'No, surely not. Her car is a darker red than that,' I lied.

'It's Sam, it's Sam. Yyyyessss,' screamed Muffs, who ran to a pale red car.

'Mind the cars, mate,' I advised.

Snow Man, who had been duck hunting out of season, joined Martin at the pale red car and started that wobbly-head-almost-reaching-his-bottom bendy thing that excited dogs do. Dannielle did it when we first met. If Snowy could speak, he would also be screaming Yyyyessss.

Molly, who no longer needed to wear a tent around her waist, and Danners were completely taken in. Could this be the first time these cops didn't get their men? Dannielle joined Bendy Dog and Muffs in greeting our surprise guests.

'What are you doing here?' asked Dannielle.

'I was just about to ask you the same thing,' replied Molly.

'We're treating our mums,' Steve said.

She hadn't noticed John's dad in the back seat of the car.

'You recommended this place to us if you remember, and I can see why. It's absolutely lovely. Everything I could, and have, asked for, except a mountain. But the castles make up for it.'

'Why are those screens there?' asked John, cleverly. (Not his surname, just the way he asked the question.)

'It was really windy before,' said a complicit landlord. 'They keep the breeze away from that notoriously breezy part of the canal bank where you are seated. I've seen people blown into the canal right there. [Now he's overacting as well.] Most of them have been rescued. The weather is much better than I expected so I'll remove them for you.'

Unnoticed by the sharper minds of our party, and with some difficulty whilst carrying two heavy screens, our accomplice tapped the end of his nose towards John in that *mum's the word* manner.

'That's Gordon, or Gordy lad as we call him. He's the landlord, guys. We're here that often, we are like family to him.'

'Steady on, baby, I wouldn't go that far,' said Molly. 'I didn't know his name until just then.'

'Hang on, let me see who is at the tiller when it comes into sight. Yes, that's him. Come on, let's go over and wave.'

'I'm coming too,' said Molly.

'And me,' said Mona. 'Do I need a lifebelt?'

Don't tempt me, I thought.

Martin and I were waving our arms off, when Dannielle noticed it. 'Lovely name for a boat that, *Freedom*. I'm sure I've mentioned that to you in the past, hun. Pity the nameplate isn't on properly, though. Spoils it a bit. It looks like it's been stuck on instead of screwed.'

Panicking and wary of complete tack failure (CTF), I shouted, 'Okay, let's eat,' and we returned to our seats.

The boat with two names slipped on into the afternoon sun to the theme tune from *Howards' Way*, with its skipper renaming her for the second time that day.

John's dad was sitting next to him. 'Hi, Bill,' I said. 'Nice to see you. Happy birthday. How are you, mate?'

'I'm okay, thanks, Steve. Nice to see you too. I think that boat used to be called *Hope*. That tatty new nameplate was just about hanging on there.'

Well, I thought, at least I've got him talking. Although I wished he'd shut up, and thank goodness the younger females had gone off to the loo before his potentially deceit-busting observation was broadcast.

Never understood that. The toilet thing, not the nameplate, obviously. Can you imagine me asking John if he fancied going to the toilet with me. I ask you! Well, I just have.

Introductions followed and there was a very nice, cordial, lazy sunny day. A no-wind (where we were), completely-oblivious-feel-to-proceedings kind of afternoon. Until.

Contrary to an earlier instruction, I heard my mum say, 'Really, I love *Riverdance*. Please show me, Mona,' to Flatley.

She was up in a Flatley flash, doing whatever the opposite of gliding is, across the grass. No safety net.

'Why is Nanna Flatley limping around like a teapot, Dad?'

'And her spout is too straight,' added Sam.

'Tricky one that, boys. It's something that she has been practising at home, guys.'

'Well, she hasn't practised hard enough,' observed Sam.

'Or long enough,' supported Martin, lifting an actual teapot as evidence. (Hands to mouths.)

Diners on table 24 were overheard.

'Sad to see that. I hope the bus she arrived in was one of the ones we donated towards.'

A second. 'I hope she still knows the difference between grass and water.'

Mona returned, perfectly dry, backstage, to ill-deserved applause from ourselves and the windblown tables 19–25 inclusive.

Later, after a really tasty lunch, and feeling relieved that I wasn't wearing any foodstuff, I felt rather pleased with myself.

The OAPs (like The Three Degrees without any singing and with a female missing) were huddled together so that they could hear one another, comparing hearing aids. That was proving problematical because when they took their hearing aids out to show one another, they couldn't hear what the other two were saying.

Molly and Dannielle were talking baby stuff, and John winked at me with that cheers-mate wink, great day, fooled them, good-job wink that men use. Not the do-you-fancy-coming-to-the-toilet- with-me wink. That's slower.

'Okay, who's for the swings?' I asked.

'Me me me me me,' shouted John.

As Snowy risked having his teeth knocked out by two largely air-based seven-year-old yobbos, who were on the swings, John, who had earlier refused to get off the see-saw when asked by a parent of a five-year-old, or thereabouts, came sulking over to me.

'I take my hat off to you, Stevo. What a day. My dad is talking, and looks comfortable on the outside at least. Flatley has performed *I'm a Little Teapot* to an appreciative audience, or more accurately half a dozen pic-a-nic tables, and your mum has made them both laugh with her anecdotes and stories. The one about the spinsters' club was very funny. Although I don't think she knows it's funny. The nameplate thing was amazing. What a bit of luck that you and Shaun were former workmates and that he was moored up here today. What are the chances of that?'

'Million to one, I think he said.' I said, 'Good old Shauners. I miss him.'

I am a genius, I thought. Even my mate, a man renowned for his work on the downside of misleading people and fibbing in general, was, just like all of them, completely oblivious. Perhaps his proposed paper entitled *How to spot a mis-leader,* or in my case a silly mis-leader, was a tad inappropriate in view of his perception absence regarding the boat's owner.

I have to say that, putting aside the subterfuge, the deceit, the lies, the embarrassment and most importantly, the cost, obviously, we had all enjoyed a really pleasant friend, family, noisy kids and dog afternoon. I will definitely set up something else in the future because that is the way my misleading mind works, and as the day proved – I was good at it.

Chapter 55

That evening, my mum rang to thank Danny and I for a lovely meal, and a lovely day to boot. She ended with, 'Let's do it again soon, when I'm not at the spinsters' club, obviously.'

Mona rang Dannielle to say that it was wonderful to play in front of an appreciative audience for once, who could hear, and were there voluntarily, and that, like Mum, she had had a lovely time.

'What does it mean,' Mona asked before laughing, 'when people slap their hands together, dear? New one on me. Ha ha.'

John's dad rang him to say that he had surprised himself by how long he had managed to spend in other people's company, and, also surprisingly, how much he'd enjoyed it. He was at pains to point out, however, apparently, that (one) John's squealing, overexcited me-me-me exhibition and (two) his far-from-adult-running action had embarrassed him, and perhaps worst (three), the incident at the see-saw that saw him telling that perfectly reasonable parent that he was going to tell me (his daddy) about it.

Molly rang to reveal top-secret gossip that she had been told in the strictest confidence by her friend Judy, who didn't want to be named, about the underdressed tight-fitting young hussy who flaunts round the school and Tesco, like a PE teacher on a naughty website.

Danny fought briefly with her loyalty towards her informant before telling me what the town crier had revealed.

'That's probably because she *is* a PE teacher, Danners, who perhaps likes the sandwiches or the easy meals at Tesco. Two genuine, unmissable hussy traits, mind. Any more on the website at all?'

'Behave yourself, she's only about twenty.'

'Sorry, sorry. Did Molly say which Tesco by the way, out of interest? A second opinion might help. There are two Tescos and one Morrisons, I think, within walking or, more likely in her case, rhythmic jogging distance from the school.'

'You should refer yourself to whichever body examines misconduct in your company. They must have a file on you.' (They do.)

'Naughty Mummy,' I said. 'You have to use the word *alleged* before misconduct, until they inevitably find against me.'

Do you know, after what has seemed like a succession of recent, let's say, unwelcome events, my life was enjoying a spell of welcomence. (I know it's not a word, but it should be.) Summer was here and that felt good. I occurred to me that the perpetual summer skies were buckled with soft clouds and that they sometimes flare up in a luminous neon blue when the mood takes them. Also, I mused, summer is nature's treasure trove. The fields are laden with goldenrod-yellow flowers, and silver-washed fritillaries carry their bushels of pollen carefully.

Fortunately, a short course of tablets stopped me thinking this way last time it happened. I still had some left. I would take some.

Chapter 56

'**G**ood weekend, Steve?'

'One of the best actually, Bethington.'

After revealing the events at the Shady Oak, I boasted that I had completely bamboozled the famous crime-solving, never-before-bamboozled Cagney and Lacy and a mate who had written and published authoritative articles on how to avoid being bamboozled.

A voice from behind me said, 'A typically modest claim there, Hannibal, from a man who struggles with the quick crossword in the *Express*. Did you read how to do that in one of those weirdly named books you read, like that one titled possibly, eventually, or something like that, that I saw on your desk one time. I ask you. I just have, actually.'

The smug sense-of-achievement feeling was difficult to dismiss, partly because it was the first time I had felt it, and therefore didn't know how to dismiss it.

The day passed uneventfully thereafter and I drove home, free from pick-up duties again, whistling the rarely aired whistling version of *Simply the Best*, by whistling Tina Turner. The same feeling left me soon after Martin went to bed.

'What a day yesterday was, hun,' said Danners.

'Wasn't it, full of surprises, eh,' I said, smugly.

'Mmm. Molly and I were talking about it on the phone earlier. Gordon the landlord, owner no doubt of a gopher of the same name, had tapped the end of his nose towards Molly at the bar yesterday and said, "Don't worry, mum's the word."'

Amateur, I thought. Not going there again.

'Well, that started us thinking.'

Oh no, I thought. Thanks very much, Gordon the Gopher, masterspy.

'When I was clearing the car out earlier, I found a half-empty packet of Blu Tack in the boot, and a tin of something called glue-tac. One of the strongest waterproof adhesives available to boat builders, apparently.'

Amateur, I thought about myself.

'Then I found a note from a Graham person which read, *Best I could do in the time available, Steve. Good luck.*'

What is worse than amateur, I thought about myself.

'Thinking back to Molly's arrival, do you remember, in the light red car that you have seen a million times, which has that annoying, distracting pair of dice hanging from the mirror and bearing private number plates MO47 LLY. Do you remember what you said?'

'I remember being dazzled by the sun when they arrived,' I gulped.

'You said that Molly's car was a darker red than the one you had seen a million times.'

'Easy mistake to make,' I said out loud.

Schoolboy error, I had to concede inside. I needed a solicitor.

'There's more,' continued a now menacing Jimmy Cricket KC.

'The screens that surrounded us, or more accurately hid us, were in a place that was positively calm and tranquil compared to the comparative howling gale that tables 19–25 were battling against.'

No comment, I thought, as she read from her notes.

'Moving on to the nameplate.' (Pause) She was using the classic barristers' pause, prepare, pounce approach to witnesses from the other side. No doubt that a PPP reminder was in her notes.

'In a day, as you have admitted earlier, *full* of surprises, a boat with one of my two favourite boat names is moored just metres from our tables, *and … and …* you knew the owners. What are the chances of that?

'I'm grateful to John's dad,' she added, 'for pointing out that the boat, formally known as *Hope*, appeared to have been recently renamed. I used to love *Howards' Way*.

'You missed a chance you would never have missed if you really knew someone when you didn't call Nicky, Nickers. Damning that.

'And finally the conversation about the difference between coincidence and fate on the journey home. Overkill in retrospect, don't you think?'

Cagney and Lacey had got their man as usual. I awaited the judges' comments before sentence.

'I ask for leniency,' I said. 'Plead, actually.'

'Now,' said the judge, 'I've taken into account your previous poor conduct, your utterly childish sense of humour, your appalling bamboozling skills, the decision to act with two other accused, the admission in another courtroom from the one known to you as John, to conspire in legal terms, with another thirty-two-year-old child, himself seen making a never-before-seen scene over a see-saw, or more accurately whilst seen sitting on a see-saw, and an indiscreet pub owner, dismissed by MI5 for indiscretions, who gave us our first clue.'

She placed a black handkerchief on her head.

'In passing sentence, it gives me no pleasure, but it is my duty [here we go], to announce that the crime played out yesterday in front of vulnerable members of the public, including three tipsy OAPs, was one of the most lovely things imaginable. You are nuts, immature and sometimes completely unfathomable, Stevo, but I love you, loads, you big lump.'

Well, convicted and vindicated at the same time, I thought.

'Physio outfit, Doctor, love?' she asked.

There you are. Right there. Another one of those occasions when a woman asks you and tells you simultaneously in a question.

'Okay,' I said compliantly. 'Let's get it over with.'

Chapter 57

Well, an update for you. Thank you so much for sticking with me.

Work is going well and, confidentially (please don't tell Molly), a promotion is in the air. Soon.

Danners is as happy as a spring lamb, which made me feel bad about last Sunday's meal. Complaint here, though, she hasn't worn the physio outfit much recently. Call me selfish if you like. She hasn't had the need to make up with or to me recently. Sadly.

Molly's pregnancy is continuing very well. As is her amazing friendship with Danners. Mollers and their baby girl are in great shape.

John is ten pages into his book, bought for him by Molly, entitled *How to be a Grown-Up.* There are lots of pictures in it, but he's finding it hard to follow, apparently.

His dad ... is okay. No better than that. He sometimes talks about the Shady Oak.

My mum is now president of the spinsters' club, largely because she was the only candidate. She has been invited to talk to similar clubs around North Yorkshire, under the banner *Next stop Westminster, for this 'ere spinster.*

Flatley is pleased that her acting pals 'The Padside Players' and the nearby, famed 'Darrowby Dramatics Group', including a promising young talent named Oliver Herriot, have combined in a futile attempt to raise their appallingly low standards and attract an audience. Without success to date, however. Most of them couldn't act the goat.

Martin is nearly eight years old, and is now allowed to wander ear muffs-free around the house. He is pleased that his ears have remained flat to his head. He has a new cap that fits him and a much better grasp of the suitability of words.

Sam has made a further attempt to join Martin on the staff notice board, but the word willy was deemed below the threshold by the judging panel, which included the fireman-obsessed Mrs Goodman. She has a very low threshold, apparently.

Snow Man is Snow Man and we love him for it. Missie the poodle is a little nervous around him. Good lad, Snow Man.

Well, you're up to date. Goodbye to you, reader. Thank you for reading a book that has given me great pleasure in writing. My sincere thanks go to David Onyett of The Choir Press, who has encouraged and advised me throughout. And, of course, my children Shelley and Ben for being Shelley and Ben.

Oh, just before I go, John, Molly and Sam were here earlier. I watched as Dannielle whispered something in Molly's ear. Someone had scored at Wembley again and they were doing that footballer thing.

Is she? you ask.

Obviously, you would say, if you could see her.

Fourteen weeks actually, and our little baby girl is doing very well, thank you.

Farewell, from a very proud man.